miss O
& friends ™

ROOM FOR
ONE MORE

miss O & friends™

ROOM FOR
ONE MORE

By Harlie, with
Devra Newberger Speregen

Illustrated by Hermine Brindak

Watson-Guptill Publications/New York

For Michele and Ilanit and their "newest bergers."

Senior Editor: Julie Mazur
Project Editor: Cathy Hennessy
Production Manager: Joseph Illidge

First published in 2006 by Watson-Guptill Publications,
a division of VNU Business Media, Inc.,
770 Broadway, New York, NY 10003
www.watsonguptill.com

Cataloging-in-Publication Data available from the Library of Congress

ISBN-13: 978-0-8230-2947-1
ISBN: 0-8230-2947-6

Printed in the U.S.A.

First printing 2006

Contents

juliette   isabella   miss O   harlie   justine

Meet the group!

Welcome to
Miss O and Friends!

When I, the real Juliette, was ten years old, I created the basis for Miss O and Friends. It all started when I was on the way home from a family vacation. I was bored, so I tried to think of something fun to do. The only thing that I could really do was draw. I borrowed some paper from my mom and started to draw "cool girls." I gave them to my mom and, like all mothers, she told me they were nice and put them in her purse. Little did she know that one day these drawings would turn into something much bigger.

Years later, with the help of my mom, my sister, and some friends, we started to create the Miss O girls. At first, it was just something fun to do—we'd play around on the computer creating all sorts of stuff. It wasn't until we realized that girls really liked our characters that the idea came to us to start a company. Now, thanks to girls like you, the Miss O and Friends website (www.missoandfriends.com) has become the most popular tween site ever!

The five Miss O girls are based on girls just like you and me, and they all possess important values and do things they love to do. This series of books features a story from each of the girls. Harlie narrates this book—the second one in the series. We hope you enjoy it!

ROOM FOR ONE MORE

Chapter 1
Manga Mania Birthday

"Oh my gosh!" My best friend Miss O's voice bounced off the walls in the quiet gallery of the Museum of Modern Art in New York City and echoed through the hallways.

I made a face at her from across the room. "Hey, girlfriend!" I whispered harshly. "Use your indoor voice, please!"

Miss O bit her bottom lip. "Ooops!" she whispered back to me. "Sorry, Harlie! But you have to come see this! I mean, this could totally be you!"

Next to Miss O stood my other three BFFs: Juliette, Isabella, and Justine. They were all nodding like bobblehead dolls and waving me over enthusiastically.

I moved away from the 1960s Japanese cartoon Astro Boy exhibit I'd been enjoying and headed across the room to where my friends were checking out a life-size manga mural. The manga and anime exhibit at the

MoMA was all part of a larger comic book art exhibit. "Manga" is a wildly popular form of Japanese comic book art.

It also happens to be my obsession!

Juliette, Miss O's older sister, motioned for me to walk faster.

"Hurry!" she called out in a loud whisper. "You totally need to check this out! It does look like you!" she agreed. "Except this girl has a cat as her sidekick. You would never have a cat for a sidekick, right, Harlie?"

I grinned. My peeps knew me so well!

"No way!" I replied. "If I were a manga superhero, my sidekick would definitely be a dog."

"Like Rocky!" Isabella offered.

"Absolutely," I replied, picturing my lovable little Maltese, Rocky, as my superhero sidekick. The image cracked me up. "Can't you just see Rocky trying to help fight crime?" I asked my friends with a chuckle.

We all laughed harder, picturing Rocky doing anything that involved running or jumping. You should know my adorable little dog is truly overweight. I mean, not only couldn't he help fight crime, he could barely roll over on his back for a belly rub!

I considered the manga superhero girl that my best friends thought looked like me. True, we both had the same black spiky hair. And we were both Asian. (I'm Chinese.) And, I'm proud to say, we both had some pretty strong muscles. (Mine come from being a gymnast.) But that was where the similarities ended. Or at least, so I thought.

"See the short black spiky hair?" Isabella pointed out. "That's exactly how you wear your hair, Harlie!"

"But look at her outfit," I commented. "I would never, ever wear lime green pants with a silver shirt!"

Miss O let out a laugh. "That's true," she said. "You have much more fashion sense than that, Harlie. But look at her army boots! Those have your name written all over them!"

"Yes! You're right, Miss O!" my friend Justine said. "I can totally see Harlie wearing boots like those."

I laughed. I did have boots just like the manga superhero girl we were looking at. I loved wearing clunky, high boots like that. They're so funky.

"What are you girls looking at?" a voice behind us suddenly asked.

We all turned to find my mom and Juliette and Miss O's mom standing behind us, holding shopping bags from the MoMA gift shop. The other girls' moms were across the room, sitting on a bench chatting.

"It's Japanese comic art," Isabella told her. "They call it 'manga,'" she began to explain.

My mother and I let out a laugh as Isabella started explaining what manga was. Why did we laugh? Because my mother already knew everything there was to know about Japanese manga—my father and I had been huge fans for years!

"Oh, you mean Japanese manga, a term meaning 'whimsical picture,' coined in 1815 by the artist Hokusai, best known for his famous woodblock prints 'One Hundred Views of Mt. Fuji?'" my mother asked innocently. "*That* Japanese manga?"

Isabella blushed. "Uh, yes," she replied. "I guess you've heard of it."

"Hello? Earth to Isabella?" I joked. "She is my mother, after all!"

Izzy grinned. "Right. Duh," she said. "I guess all anyone would have to do was take one step into your bedroom and they'd know all about manga and comics!"

"That's okay, Isabella," my mother said with a smile. "I was just kidding around with you. I'm happy to hear you like the exhibit."

"Oh, it's way cool!" Miss O chimed in. I watched as she tied her sweatshirt around her waist and inspected the mural more closely. "But do you think this character is in the style of Tezuka?" she asked my mother and me.

My eyes widened in astonishment. "Miss O! How do you know about Tezuka?" I asked.

"Hey, I pay attention!" Miss O proclaimed proudly.

My mother smiled. "Well, I'm very impressed, Olivia!" she exclaimed. (Only Miss O's friends call her 'Miss O,' a nickname she's had since she was a little kid. Most grown-ups call her by her name, Olivia.)

"Thank you," Miss O replied.

"Hmmmm," Juliette remarked slyly, "so you didn't see where it's written right here on the wall next to the art? 'In the twentieth century,'" she read, "'Tezuka Osamu was known throughout the world as the father of manga. Many artists followed Tezuka's style.'"

Miss O blushed. "Well, okay. Yes. You caught me," she said sheepishly. "But still, I do pay attention!"

I laughed and put my arm around her shoulders. "I'm just glad you're not bored to tears here," I told her.

Miss O pulled her blonde hair into a ponytail and quickly wrapped a hair band around it to hold it in place. She did it so fast that if you didn't know her as well as I did, you would think her hair band had appeared out of nowhere! But I knew better. I knew Miss O always kept a few hair bands around her wrist, and sometimes even a scrunchie. ("For hair emergencies," she always said.)

"No way," she said. "MoMA rocks!"

Miss O is definitely my most "fun" friend! Whenever we hang out, all we do is laugh! Like, last week, when we were hanging out at her house pretending to audition for *American Idol*. Miss O kept trying to sing a "serious" song, but every time she sang the word "special," she would spit a little! I nearly busted a gut laughing so hard. It was hilarious.

"Ready to move on?" my mother asked us.

We all nodded. Then we left the manga and anime part of the exhibit and followed my mother and the other moms down the stairs, heading for the next comic book art display.

As I flew down the steps two at a time, I was so glad I'd decided to have my birthday at the museum with just my very best, closest friends. I was having so much fun! I only hoped they didn't think spending the day at the museum for my birthday was lame.

In all honesty, I did check out other places for my birthday celebration before deciding on MoMA. Like the dance center around the corner from my building, the Flips Club (my gymnastics club), Starbucks (hey, I love mocha lattes!), the Plaster Palace—all of which would have been cool, I guess. But when my mom told me about the new comic book art exhibit at

MoMA, I knew it was exactly how I wanted to spend my eleventh birthday!

"Harlie, this is just so awesome," Justine said. She pushed a long, brown banana curl away from her eyes and tucked it behind an ear. "I'm enjoying this a lot! When I lived in England, we used to go to museums all the time."

In case you were wondering, Justine is American, but she has lived in other countries all over the world. She is what some people call an "army brat." That means one of her parents (her father) is in the United States Army and her family lives on army bases wherever her father is stationed. Justine has lived in England and Germany, but now she lives in Westchester, New York, on an army base a few towns over from the Sage School, the private school where we all go.

Justine is awesome. She's so, so nice and so, so smart! Having lived in so many different places, she, like, knows everything about everything! But she's not a know-it-all or anything like that. In fact, she's really shy. When you first meet her, you think maybe she doesn't know stuff because she's usually pretty quiet. Then you get to know her, and you watch *Who Wants to Be a Millionaire* with her on TV one day, and she surprises you by knowing the answers to the craziest questions! Like the time she knew the capital of Wales was Cardiff. I mean, who knows that stuff?

Anyway, Justine walked next to me, snapping away at everything with her camera. She usually brings her digital camera everywhere she goes, but today she had a different camera with her, one with a very large lens. I think it's because you aren't allowed to use a flash in museums. It damages the artwork or something like that.

"Did you get any pictures of the manga art?" I asked.

"I hope so," Justine said. "The lighting was okay, but I wish I could have used my flash. Anyway, maybe something will come out."

"If it does, please make copies for me!" Juliette said, coming up behind us. "Harlie, this museum is way cool!" she added as we stepped into the next area of the exhibit. "I'm already thinking about a new story I'm going to write for my creative writing project at school. A story that takes place in a museum just like this! Maybe a mystery!"

Juliette is the writer in our group of friends. She's so talented! Last year she wrote a play at school, and we all got to be in it. It was such a funny play. It was about five girls and a dog waiting in line for concert tickets. Rocky got to be in the play, too! The whole audience just cracked up when he waddled out on stage during the play. (Did I already mention Rocky is seriously fat?)

Since Juliette is a year older than the rest of us, she's in the first year of middle division at the Sage School, which is the same as being in sixth grade at public school. Miss O, Justine, Isabella, and I are all in our last year of lower division, or fifth grade.

Anyway, I was glad to hear that all of my friends were having a good time at MoMA. I was about to ask Isabella what she thought, but as we stepped inside a room filled with life-size paintings of superheroes all over the walls, I was suddenly speechless.

"Wow! This is sweet!" I gushed. For a major comic book fan like me, this was a dream come true. I was totally surrounded by larger-than-life images of all my most favorite comic book characters ever!

"And look, Harlie!" Isabella exclaimed. "It's Batman! comic book Batman—not television Batman!"

I laughed. A few years ago, Isabella would never have known the difference between Batman and Superman, let alone comic book Batman and television Batman! But now, after becoming friends with me, she'd learned enough to know that comic book characters were often very different from the movie or TV characters of the same name. Batman, for instance, is also called "The Dark Knight" in comic books. In the old TV show reruns of Batman, he's not such a dark character; instead, the Batman TV show is a comedy.

Isabella is originally from Peru. She moved here—well, not here to NYC but to Westchester, near Miss O and Juliette—when she was little, after her parents got divorced. Now she lives a few blocks from the Sage School with her mother and her stepfather.

"These are enormous!" Isabella exclaimed. Her big, brown eyes were wide with excitement as she checked out the life-size portraits. "How cool would it be to cover your bedroom walls with all these huge paintings?"

"That would be beyond awesome!" I agreed. "Can you imagine that? Batman, The Fantastic Four, Superman and don't forget my all-time favorite . . . "

"Spider-Man!" the girls all shouted in unison.

It was true. Spidey was my fave. Another obsession. Maybe it was because Spider-Man, a.k.a Peter Parker, was from Queens, New York, just a borough away from Manhattan, where I'm from. Or maybe it was because

Spider-Man is my father's favorite, too. Well, whatever the reason, I'd always felt a certain connection to Spider-Man.

Dorky, I know! But it's true. I love the Spider-Man comic books. I have hundreds of them back home in my collection. I even have the very first Spider-Man comic book ever made: *The Amazing Spider-Man* from 1963! Well, okay, truth be told it's my father's comic book. But he says he's going to give it to me one day. Right now, it's hanging on the wall in our living room in a glass shadow box. My father says it's in mint condition and worth thousands of dollars!

But anyway, at the moment, I was lost in all the life-size works of art of my favorite superheroes. They would be sweet hanging on the walls of my room at home. "Maybe they sell posters in the gift shop or something," I said. "I could buy a few and hang them up in my room."

"Or maybe—" Miss O added, letting her voice trail off mysteriously. I shot a look over at her and noticed that familiar twinkle in her eye. The twinkle she got when she was having one of her brilliant brainstorms!

"What is it, Miss O?" I asked excitedly.

My friend grinned. "Maybe," she repeated, "we could paint a life-size mural right on your wall ourselves!"

I stopped for a moment and considered that. If anyone could paint a life-size mural of a superhero, it would be Miss O. She's a super-talented artist. She even has her own art studio set up in her bedroom!

But I thought about my bedroom back home in the Upper West Side loft I lived in with my parents. It was a very large loft, but my bedroom was kind of on the small side. Plus, I didn't have a lot of wall space in my room, considering one wall was all windows overlooking the street, another whole wall had closet doors on it, and another wall had my dressers up against it. The only sort of "open" wall space there was had the door to my room right in the middle of it and some built-in shelves on it for my books and stuff.

"That's a great idea," I told Miss O. "But I don't think there's enough wall space in my bedroom for a mural."

"Wait! I have a better idea!" Juliette exclaimed.

Everyone looked at her.

"What if we paint the mural in the Latte Lounge?" she suggested.

"Oooh, yes! And we can all help!" Isabella added, excitedly.

"That would be fun," Justine agreed.

My eyes widened and I smiled. "That's an excellent idea!" I said. The Latte Lounge is what we all called the spare bedroom in my loft where my parents let me keep my comic book collection and my electric guitar and other important stuff. I also have some beanbag chairs in there for me and my friends to hang out on when they come over. Once, last summer, I made iced mocha lattes for everyone and we hung out on the beanbags pretending we were at a coffee bar. Miss O had joked that it was like our own, private Latte Lounge, and that's what we've called it ever since.

"Oh my god!" Miss O suddenly exclaimed. "I have an even better better idea!"

"A better better idea?" I asked with a giggle.

Miss O's blue eyes were wide and sparkling with excitement as she nodded. "Instead of painting just any superhero in the Latte Lounge," she said, "how about if you create an original superhero for me to paint?"

"A manga superhero!" Justine suggested.

I broke into a huge grin. "Wow, that is better than better," I said. "I've been wanting to do that for so long. That would be awesome!"

"Hey, and what if we wrote a whole comic book story to go with your new superhero?" Juliette chimed in. "I could write it, and you could sketch it out—you know, like in a comic book-style. Then we can send it to a publisher or something!"

"Or enter it in a contest!" Justine suggested. "And I'll take photos of everyone working on it and send them to all the newspapers in Westchester!"

The more we discussed the idea, the bigger it grew, and the more excited everyone became. Everyone had a part in the project, too, even if they couldn't draw or write. I would create the character, and Miss O would transfer it on the wall. Juliette would write the comic book story, Justine would take pictures, and Isabella offered to organize the whole project, which was a good idea because out of all of us, she was the most organized.

"Do you think your parents will let you do it?" Isabella asked, lowering her voice a bit so the moms couldn't hear us. Isabella's parents are pretty strict about a lot of things, so she is always worried about being allowed to do stuff. But my parents are the opposite—they aren't strict at all. I'm an only child, so it's just me at home. That doesn't mean I get away with anything, but it does mean I'm treated differently. My parents let me do a lot more stuff, and I hardly ever get punished or grounded, mostly because there's no one at home for me to argue or fight with!

I'm pretty much allowed to do whatever I want at home. I can stay up late (my bedtime is 10:30 p.m.) as long as I can wake up on my own for early gymnastics training. And I can eat whatever I want, too, as long as I promise to eat protein. (That's because I'm a vegetarian and I don't eat meat. Since meat has a lot of protein, my parents always insist I eat other foods with protein, like nuts and cheese and stuff.)

Lately, Mom says she thinks I've matured a lot, too. And I like that she's been treating me more grown-up lately. Like, she doesn't wait downstairs for the school bus in the afternoons anymore. She trusts me to get off the bus and go upstairs by myself, which is really great.

Anyway, my parents are very cool. I didn't think they'd have a problem with me painting a mural in the Latte Lounge, but I figured I'd ask anyway.

I found my mother in the comic book villains exhibit, which was an area of the gallery filled with art of all the bad guys from different comic book stories. It was way cool, but a little creepy, too.

"Mom?" I asked, interrupting her as she checked out a gigantic illustration of Doc Ock, a notorious villain from the Spider-Man comics.

"Pretty amazing, don't you think, Harlie?" my mother asked.

"Definitely," I agreed. "Dad would have loved this. Doc Ock is his favorite bad guy!"

My mother faced me. "You know, sweetheart, your father felt terrible about missing your birthday today."

I nodded. "I know that, Mom."

"The agency really needed him in San Francisco—there was an emergency with our top account." My parents both work for the same advertising agency in the city. Dad travels a lot, while Mom works mostly in the office or at home.

"I know that, Mom. It's okay. Really!"

My mother gave me a quick hug. "He'll make it up to you," she promised, pushing my bangs out of my eyes. (She always does that!) "Maybe you two can come back next weekend to see the exhibit again."

I smiled. That would be fun. And Dad would love it, too. If there was a bigger comic book fan than me, it was definitely my father!

"Anyway . . . Mom?" I asked.

"Yes?"

"The girls and I would like to paint a mural on the wall in the Latte Loun—, er, in the spare bedroom," I said. "Do you think that would be okay?"

My mom nodded, then spun back around toward Doc Ock and his eight enormous octopus legs. "Sure, honey. I don't see why not. You can even use your father's wall projector to transfer the image if you'd like."

"Wow! Thanks, Mom!" (I told you my parents were cool.)

"After the museum, I have a surprise for you," Mom added.

My eyes widened. "Really? What?"

"We're all going to Starbucks for mocha lattes!" she exclaimed.

"Awesome!" I cried. Mom knows how much I love mocha lattes from Starbucks. She and I have this thing, we're trying to visit every Starbucks in New York City! We keep a list of the ones we visit. There are more than one hundred and fifty in Manhattan! (So far, we've been to twenty-five of them.)

I gave her a quick kiss on the cheek and headed back toward where the girls were waiting for the word. I held up both arms as I approached them, and with a big smile, I said, "High-fives all around! Mom just gave Project Manga Mural the green light!"

Everyone high-fived. At that very moment, visions of my new comic-book superhero danced around in my head. She was a latte-drinking, crime-fighting vegetarian, who played a mean electric guitar, moved like an Olympic gymnast, looked exactly like me . . . and had a fat, little white Maltese for a sidekick.

The Upper West Side's newest superhero: Harlie Rox and her chubby Maltese Rocky!

Chapter 2

The New Kid
on the Bus

Usually, I hate waking up on Monday mornings. But today was different.

Not because it was five a.m.—I always get up at five a.m. on Mondays and Thursdays because I have gymnastics training at six a.m.

And not because today was the day I would find out if I'd made the cut for the Team USA Junior Gymnasts Classic. (Though I was pretty excited about that!)

This Monday morning was different because I had a brand-new alarm clock to wake me up. The clock Miss O and Juliette had given me for my birthday yesterday! My new clock didn't ring or buzz like a regular old alarm clock. Instead, it played a pre-recorded message. And Miss O and Juliette had personally made a special recording for me to wake up to.

Waking up at five a.m. had never been so fun!

Here's what woke me up:

> Like, totally!
> Like, wow!
> Like, get outta bed right now!
> Get up, Harlie! Get outta bed!
> Like, didn't you hear what we said?

It was so funny to hear my friends' goofy voices yelling at me to wake up that I couldn't possibly stay asleep. The funniest part was they were both laughing and screaming like lunatics when they recorded it.

So that's why this Monday morning was different. Even though it was five a.m., I woke up laughing my head off.

I dragged myself out of bed, washed up, brushed my teeth, and put on my unitard. I pulled a pair of sweats over my unitard, then rolled them over at the waist a few times to achieve the "cool factor." (That's how I always wear my sweats—rolled over at the waist so that the tags in the back show.)

At a quarter to six I was sitting on the bench by the front door, sipping my usual breakfast mocha latte and rubbing Rocky's neck as I waited for my mother to walk me over to the gym where I train.

Five minutes passed and my mother had still not emerged from her bedroom. I glanced at the clock on the wall and started to get a little antsy. It takes ten minutes to walk the two blocks to the gym, and I hate being late. You know who else hates it when I'm late? My coach!

About two years ago, I started training with Coach Ilana Saffeir, a famous gymnastics coach from Russia. I was lucky to get her to train me because she's very busy and she trains lots of kids in New York City. Some of those kids have been to the Olympics! But to be honest with you, I don't love spending two mornings a week with Coach Ilana. (Between you and me, she isn't the sweetest person in the world. Definitely not the warm and fuzzy type.)

By six o'clock, I was already late for sure. I stood up from the bench and knocked on my parents' bedroom door.

"Mom!" I called out. "What's going on? We're late!"

My mother's voice was sleepy and crackly as she called back from inside her room. "I know! Sorry, honey! I overslept! I'll be out in two minutes!"

Great. Coach Ilana was going to freak!

A few minutes later, Mom was ready. As we waited for the elevator, I happened to glance down at her feet.

"Mom!" I cried. "You still have your slippers on!"

My mother nodded. "I know. No big deal," she said. "No one will notice."

"I noticed!" I said. "Come on, Mom! That's so embarrassing!"

My mother yawned. "Relax, Harlie," she said gently. "I promise, no one will notice. My slippers look like shoes anyway. Let's just walk quickly and get you there as soon as possible. I'm so sorry—I'm just not myself this morning!"

As we hurried past the doorman and out onto the street, I quickly checked to make sure there were no other kids around to see my mother's ridiculous slippers (that did not, mind you, look like shoes). Luckily, it was pretty quiet in front of my building.

Together, we hurried down Columbus Avenue toward my gymnastics school, the Flips Club.

"I'll talk to Coach Ilana for you," my mother said as we walked inside. "It's my fault you're late."

"Okay. Good. Thanks," I said, feeling a little relieved. Coach Ilana would freak out on my mother!

When we got inside, we hurried upstairs to the training gym. I imagined the sour expression on Coach Ilana's face as we walked through the double doors into the training gym.

But when my mom pushed open the doors and we stepped inside, you can imagine how surprised I was to see Coach Ilana smiling!

"Harlie!" she called out to us with a wave.

Mom and I exchanged looks.

"You made it, Harlie!" she cried. "One more stop, then you're on your way to the Classic!"

My eyes widened. My mother threw her arms around me and squeezed me hard.

"I . . . I made it? Really?" I asked.

Coach Ilana was making her way across the gym, walking toward me with her arms wide open.

Oh my god, she wants a hug.

Before I knew it, she was hugging me. Then she hugged Mom!

"I knew it!" she said. "You were really the best one in your level. Are those slippers?" she asked my mother.

I groaned.

Mom flashed me a quick look. "Uh, no. These are shoes," she mumbled.

"Wow, that's great!" I finally managed to say. I was still in shock that I'd actually made it, but it was starting to sink in.

The Team USA Junior Gymnasts Classic is a big gymnastics meet that's held every two years in Miami, Florida. It's very hard to make it to the Classic—you have to try out twice. First, I had to compete against all the girls in my level—the seventh—at the Flips Club. Only the highest scoring gymnast moves on. That's me!

Next step is to qualify for the Classic, which means I'll have to do my floor routine for the Team USA judges and compete against the winners from other gymnastics clubs in New York City. The top three girls with the highest scores will then qualify to compete in the Classic.

"So we need to get cracking on your floor routine," Coach Ilana announced. (She had suddenly transformed back to her old gruff self.) "Time to get moving! Go stretch!"

I hugged Mom again and headed to stretch out. This was just so amazing! I couldn't stop smiling. The Team USA Junior Gymnasts Classic was a very prestigious event—and now I was this close to being in it! At the moment, there was just one floor program that stood between me and Miami!

Back home that morning, I was so excited I had to call Dad in San Francisco to tell him the news. (I probably should have waited until later though, because it was only about four in the morning over there!) He sounded sleepy, but he was really happy for me.

"I'll be home Tuesday night, Sugar Plum!" he said. "We'll go out to celebrate. You pick the place!"

"Oh, sure!" I said with a laugh. "That's because you know I'll pick BOP!" BOP (Brick Oven Pizza) is my favorite restaurant on the Upper West Side. It's my dad's favorite, too.

"Of course!" he replied. "If we let your mother pick, we'd be eating at—"

"The coffee shop on Broadway!" I finished for him.

"I like the coffee shop!" my mother called out from the kitchen.

"Yuck!" I called back to her. Then to Dad, "Listen, Dad. Mom wore her slippers in public this morning."

Dad laughed into the phone. "Oh, no, Harlie. That's terrible! You know I count on you to make sure Mom doesn't embarrass the family while I'm away on business!"

"Sorry, Dad! But I thought you should know!"

We made a few more jokes about Mom, then I hung up the phone and cartwheeled all the way to my room. I was in such a great mood! Rocky followed me down the hall, waddling as best as he could to keep up with me. I really need to put that dog on a diet.

In my room, I changed out of my gym clothes and got ready for the shower. Wait until the girls all heard my news! They were going to bust! Maybe they could all come down to Miami with me this summer if I made it to the Classic. They could come watch me compete, then we could hang out in Miami Beach. How fun would that be?

I decided I couldn't wait to tell them. Before I got in the shower, I sent out a mass e-mail.

> **To:** gOalgirl, jujuBEE, JUSTme713, IzzyBELLA
> **Time:** 7:03 a.m.
> **CC:**
> **Subject:** GUESS WHAT????
>
> HUGE news!!!! BIGGER than HUGE. COLOSSAL!
> DOORZ...first thing! :)
>
> Harlie.

The "doorz" was what we called the doors by the gym at school. Since practically forever, we've been meeting by the "doorz" in the morning, just to hang for a few minutes before school started.

I showered quickly and got dressed for school. Today was not a gym day, so I could wear whatever I wanted. I pulled on my favorite jeans and a long-sleeved black tee. Then I layered the *American Idol* short-sleeved tee that Justine had given me for my birthday yesterday over the long-sleeved tee. Finally, I slipped into my favorite black high-top boots and I rolled up the bottom of the legs of my jeans.

I was ready to rock!

Luckily, I keep my hair short, short, so it doesn't take too much time to do in the mornings when I'm in a rush to catch the bus. This morning I towel-dried it, then used some gel to put in a few spikes on the top. I grabbed my jacket and my book bag and raced out the door.

"Bye, Mom!" I called out as I left. "I'm going to the bus!"

"See you later, hon!" Mom called back.

Downstairs, I waited for the Sage School bus. I stood under the awning to my building and told Steve the doorman my big news.

"Harlie! That is superfantastic!" Steve said. "Good for you! Your parents must be so proud."

I nodded. "Yup."

"We're all going to be watching you at the Olympics one day!" Steve added. Just then, he headed back toward the glass doors to the building and pulled one open. "Good morning, Mrs. Kappel," he said as a pretty woman in a business suit walked outside, holding hands with a little girl. "And good morning, Lanie! How are you today?"

"Hi, Steve!" the little girl said. "I'm fine."

Mrs. Kappel smiled at the doorman, then she and her daughter walked over to me.

"Are you Harlie?" Mrs. Kappel asked me.

"Yes," I told her, wondering how she knew my name. I had seen her in the building before, but there were hundreds of people in my building and I didn't know everybody's name.

"Oh, great, great, great!" she said with a smile. "I'm Shane Kappel, and this is my daughter, Lanie."

I glanced down at the little girl, who was staring back at me as if I had two heads.

"Um, hi," I said.

"Lanie is starting at the Sage School today," Mrs. Kappel went on. "Kindergarten. The school administrator told me there was another Sage student in our building."

I nodded. "Yes. I'm in lower division at Sage, too," I told her. "But this is my last year in lower division. Then I move up to middle division," I added proudly.

"Well, Harlie, you don't know how happy, happy, happy I am to meet you! And that Lanie has someone to ride the bus with every day!"

I managed a half-smile, wondering why Mrs. Kappel repeated some words three times like that. I was also wondering if she actually thought I was going to ride the bus to school with a kindergartener, because I wasn't sure I wanted to—

"I was really just so, so, so anxious about sending Lanie to school on a bus so far away," Mrs. Kappel went on, "but I heard such great things about Sage."

I nodded.

"So do you mind, Harlie?" she asked. "Can you stay with my Lanie on the bus so I know she'll be okay? Maybe look after her a little? I would really, really, really appreciate it!"

I glanced down at Lanie, who was staring at my boots.

"Why are your pants rolled up like that?" Lanie asked me.

"Oh. Um, because I like how it looks," I told her.

"Why?" she asked again.

Sheesh! "Because I just do," I said.

"Now, Lanie, promise me you'll behave and stay in your seat on the bus," Mrs. Kappel said to her daughter. She zipped Lanie's winter jacket all the way up to her neck, then flipped up the hood and pulled the drawstrings closed and tied them. Lanie's little head slowly disappeared.

"Mom!" Lanie protested.

"She needs to go straight to the main office," Mrs. Kappel told me. "And they'll take her from there to meet her teacher. Okay, Harlie? Do you mind?"

I shook my head. Did I have a choice?

Finally the bus pulled up in front of the building. I noticed Mrs. Kappel's eyes were a little teary as she hugged Lanie goodbye.

"Have a great first day!" she called out.

"Bye, Mom!" Lanie called back as she climbed onto the bus.

"Don't worry, Mrs. Kappel," I said. "I'll get her to the main office."

Mrs. Kappel smiled at me. "Thank you, thank you, thank you!"

I found Lanie on the bus, trying to undo her jacket and hood. I sat down in the seat next to her.

"I know where the office is," Lanie said to me, matter-of-factly. "My mom showed it to me a million times."

"Well, she asked me to take you there, so if it's okay, I'll walk with you there this time."

Lanie shrugged. "Okay," she said. "How come you don't have to wear a hood, Harlie?" she asked.

"Because I don't," I told her.

"But how come?" she asked again.

"I just don't have to wear one," I said.

"My mother makes me wear a hood even if it's sunny," Lanie grumbled. "How come your hair sticks up like that?" she asked.

I felt my spiky bangs with my hand. "Um, because I gel it," I told her.

"Why?"

"So it sticks up!"

"How come you have a bag like that and not a backpack like mine?" she asked, holding up a Care Bears backpack.

I laughed to myself, thinking about how funny it would be if I showed up to school with a Care Bears backpack. I let Lanie see my new messenger-style bag, which is from the Gap.

"Because I like this bag," I told her.

"Why?" she asked.

Boy, this kid sure asked a lot of questions!

"Just because!" I said, feeling slightly irritated at having to answer them all so early in the morning.

"What's your teacher's name?" Lanie asked.

"Mr. Lauro," I told her.

"A mister?" Lanie asked.

I nodded. "Yes."

"Is he nice?" she asked.

"Very nice," I replied.

"My teacher is Mrs. Biscari," Lanie said. "It is not Mrs. Biscotti," she added.

That made me chuckle. "No, it's not," I said.

"What number is your classroom?" she asked.

I sighed. "Two-fourteen."

"Mine is one-eleven. Is that close to your room?"

"No."

"What did you bring for lunch?" Lanie asked.

I rubbed my eyes. "I'm buying lunch today," I told her.

"Why?" she asked.

Oh, brother! Doesn't she know any other words? "Because I like maca- roni and cheese," I said in exasperation. I slumped and put my knees up on the seat in front of me. "Listen, Lanie. Maybe you can stop asking so many questions? I had to wake up really early this morning and I'm very tired."

"How come?" she asked.

"Lanie!"

"Wait! Just one more!" she pleaded. "Please? How come you had to wake up early?"

I sighed again. "Because I take gymnastics in the morning and I can only train early."

"Why?"

I slid even further down in my seat.

Please, Mr. Bus Driver, I prayed silently in my head. Can't you drive any faster?

Chapter 3
I Don't Need Another BFF

At lunchtime later that day, I practically flew all the way from my classroom to the cafeteria. The girls were going to kill me! I had been the one to ask them to meet at the "doorz" this morning, then I was the one who didn't show up!

If only Lanie hadn't asked me to wait with her at the main office. My plan had been to drop her off, then high-tail it over to the "doorz" to meet my buds and tell them the big news. But when I saw the pathetic expression on Lanie's little face—she looked really scared standing in the office all alone—I just couldn't bear to leave her by herself.

So I stayed while we waited for the school administrator. We sat on a little bench by the front desk and I answered another trillion questions.

Why do the buses drop us off at the side of the school?
Why is the office so crowded?
Why is there a mural on the wall?
Why are there two cafeterias?
WhyWhyWhyWhyWhyWhyWhyWhyWhyWhyWhyWhyWhy?

My brain was hurting by the time the administrator showed up to take Lanie to class. Anyway, when I finally got to the "doorz," the girls were gone.

In the cafeteria, I stood on line to buy lunch and gazed across the large room toward the table where my friends and I always sit. Justine was already there and she caught me waving to her. She gave me a big shrug and a look that said, "Where were you this morning?" So I indicated to her that I would explain everything in a minute.

I bought my mac-and-cheese, paid for my lunch, and headed for the table. Miss O and Isabella had just arrived too—Juliette wasn't coming because she eats in a different cafeteria with the older kids in middle division.

"So, what gives, Harlie?" Miss O asked. "Where were you this morning? We waited by the 'doorz' forever! I was almost late for the Hinter Monster!"

"Ugh! I'm so sorry, Miss O!" I said sympathetically. Miss O's teacher, Mrs. Hintermeister, was really strict and had this thing about being even one second late for her class. "But I have a good reason," I explained as I set my lunch tray down on the table and opened my carton of orange juice. "I was sort of babysitting this little kindergarten kid."

"Huh?" Isabella asked. "What kindergarten kid?"

I told the girls all about Lanie from my building, and all about how it was her first day at Sage, and how her mom had asked me to keep an eye on her, yada, yada, yada.

"So I couldn't just leave her at the office," I went on. "I mean, you should have seen her face!"

"No problem, Harl," Justine said. "We would have done the same thing. But come on already! Tell us your big news! We've been dying all day!"

The girls looked at me anxiously, but I had just stuffed a forkful of mac-and-cheese in my mouth and I was chewing.

"Hmphagog," I mumbled.

Miss O rolled her eyes. "Sheesh! You're making us nuts!"

I smiled as I chewed, trying to look as apologetic as possible. The girls watched me chew, waiting for me to swallow. Finally, I did.

"Okay!" I announced, licking my lips. "Sorry about that! But I was really hungry. I only had a mocha latte this morning and—"

"Ahhhhhh!" Isabella cried. "Would you just tell us already?"

"I came in first. I'm moving up to the qualifying round!" I blurted out.

The girls all gasped. Miss O's smile was as wide as can be. "You mean Miami?" she asked.

I nodded, piercing my fork into some more mac-and-cheese, trying to act as if this were just a plain old regular moment.

Meanwhile, Miss O jumped up from her seat and threw her arms around my neck. "Harlie! That is so ultra-awesome!" she cried.

Justine and Isabella got up, too, to give me a hug.

"I can't believe it!" Justine said. "Out of all the gymnasts at your level?"

I grinned. "Yup!"

"And now what?" Isabella asked. "When do you find out if you qualify for the Classic?"

"On Thursday night," I told them. "I have to perform my floor exercise routine for the judges and get scored. I'll find out a few days later if I placed high enough to qualify. If I qualify, it's off to Miami in July!"

"Woo-hoo!" the girls all cheered. I took another bite of mac-and-cheese and leaned back in my seat feeling pretty great.

"You'll definitely qualify," Miss O said reassuringly. "You're the best gymnast I know!"

"Absolutely," Justine added. "The best!"

"And then you'll medal in the Classic!" Isabella chimed in.

"Well, I don't know about that," I told them. "But it would just be fun to go to the Classic! Can you imagine? A real national competition. In Miami!" Then I remembered my idea. "Hey, maybe you guys can come with me?"

Miss O's eyes widened. "Oh my god, that would be so awesome!" she said. "When is it?"

"It's the second week of July," I told them. "I'm going to ask my parents if you can all come. If I qualify, I mean."

"Definitely!" Isabella said. "You'll need me in Miami anyway," she added with a grin. "Everything is in Spanish there. I can translate for you."

"You mean, they don't speak English in Miami?" Miss O asked.

"Well, they do," Isabella replied. "Of course they do. But there are so many people from Latin America there, a lot of people speak Spanish."

"Then it's settled!" I said. "You'll all have to come with me! Isabella has to come to help me with Spanish, Justine has to come to take pictures, Juliette can come and write a story about me, and Miss O, you can . . ."

Miss O waited for me to finish, but I actually hadn't thought of what she could do to help me if she came to Miami with me. She frowned and took a sip of her chocolate milk. "Sounds like you don't really need me," she started to say. Then, with great dramatic flair, Miss O leaned over the table to rest her chin in her hands. When she did, her elbow landed on the end of her fork, causing the fork to flip up and send macaroni and cheese sailing into the air. We all watched as the bright orange macaroni flew through the air and landed right on my lunch tray—exactly on top of *my* macaroni and cheese!

We all exchanged amazed looks, then cracked up hysterically.

"And Miss O, you have to come with me to Miami purely for entertainment purposes!" I cried.

Miss O was laughing hard, too. "Okay, I'm up for that job!" she exclaimed.

We were still laughing when the kindergarteners appeared, walking past our table in two perfect lines behind their teachers. They all carried their lunch boxes and trays and headed for their section of the cafeteria.

That's when I heard someone calling my name. "Hi, Harlie! Hi, Harlie! Harlie? Harlie, hi! Harlie, I'm over here!"

Miss O started to giggle. "Um, Harlie?" she said. "It looks like you have a fan?"

"A fan club," Justine corrected.

I spun around in my seat to find Lanie waving at me like crazy. Worse, she was pointing me out to a dozen or so kindergarteners and they were all staring at me and waving. I had to admit she looked sort of cute with her Care Bears lunch box and a big smile on her face. But as she and all her little kindergarten buddies got closer to my table, I noticed out of the corner of my eye some fifth graders nearby were staring at me. I felt more than a little embarrassed.

"Hi, Harlie! Do you sit here every day?" Lanie asked loudly. "How come you sit over here?"

"Hi, Lanie," I said. "Um, maybe you should keep following Mrs. Biscari," I suggested. "The kindergarten kids sit over there." I pointed across the cafeteria to the tables against the opposite wall.

"But how come you get to sit here?" she asked. She looked over at my friends. "Who are they?"

"Well, after kindergarten, you don't have to sit with your class anymore," I explained. "And these are my friends, Miss O, Justine, and Isabella."

"Miss O?" Lanie asked. "She's your teacher?"

My friends all laughed.

"No, I'm Miss O," Miss O told Lanie. "I'm just a kid in fifth grade. Miss O is my nickname."

"How come?" Lanie asked.

Miss O looked at me.

"Um, I forgot to mention," I whispered, "Lanie has this habit of asking a lot of questions."

Just then, Mrs. Biscari called out to her students. "My students!" she said loudly. "Please follow me!"

"Can't I sit with you?" Lanie asked.

I suddenly felt bad for Lanie, despite the fact that every fifth grader within a ten-foot radius was hearing me talk to a loud five-year-old with a Care Bears lunch box. Still, it wasn't like I could offer for her to sit with me and my friends. It was against school rules (which I was secretly thankful for).

"No, sorry, Lanie. You can't sit with us," I said. "You have to stay with your class."

"But—" Lanie began.

"Know what?" I asked. I was kicking myself as the words came out of my mouth, regretting it from the first syllable, but I was having major sympathy pangs for this little girl, remembering how scary my first day at Sage was. I felt kind of bad for her. "Why don't we sit together on the bus home today?" I suggested. "I'll save you a seat."

Lanie's face brightened immediately. "Really?" she asked. "You'll save me a seat? Right next to you? For the whole way home?"

"Yeah, really," I said.

"Okay!" Lanie exclaimed. She was beaming. "See you later, Harlie!" she called out as she followed her class to the other side of the cafeteria. "On the bus!" she screamed. "Save me a seat! Don't forget!"

When she was gone, I turned to my friends and put my head down on the table and sighed. "Sheesh. Do you think the whole cafeteria heard?" I asked. "Why did I do that? Why did I say I'd save her a seat? What's wrong with me?"

"Nothing's wrong with you, you were just being a nice person," Justine said.

"And kind," Isabella added.

"Or you did it because you want to spend your afternoon answering questions," Miss O said with a grin.

I laughed. "Never mind!" I told them. "And by the way," I added, "you'll all be there to help me answer questions! Aren't you guys coming over after school on the bus? We're supposed to work on the manga mural and the comic book. My mom is making dinner for us."

"Yup! I'm coming," Miss O said. "My dad wrote a permission slip for me and Juliette to ride home on your bus."

"I've got my permission slip, too," Isabella said. "But my stepfather is picking me up from your house immediately after dinner." she added. "Don't forget, I have an early bedtime on school nights." She made a face to show what she thought about that.

I knew Isabella wasn't thrilled about having such a strict stepfather. He had so many rules! One rule was that Isabella had to go to bed at the same time every single night during the school week. Izzy said it was crazy because some nights she wasn't even tired and she just laid there for hours trying to fall asleep.

"Me, too," Justine chimed in. "I can't stay long either. My dad is picking me up after dinner so I can work on my science project."

"Your science project? But isn't that due like two months from now?" I asked her.

Justine nodded. "Yes," she said. "But I have to start it today. General's orders."

Justine's father was on the strict side, too. He was a famous general in the army, and sometimes Justine complained that he ran her house like an army base. She had a regular bedtime, too, but at least it was a little later than Isabella's.

Me? I could go to bed whenever I pleased. I usually went to sleep early though, because I had to get up early for gymnastics.

"Well, as long as we'll get to hang out and start the mural," I said. "I made a sketch of what I want my superhero to look like," I told Miss O. "I want to call her 'Harlie Rox'!"

"Hey, that's perfect!" Miss O said. "Great name!"

The others agreed.

"And I want her to have a sidekick," I added.

"Like Robin?" Isabella asked, referring to Batman's sidekick.

"Kind of," I said. "But I was thinking of a dog sidekick."

Justine smiled. "You mean like maybe a little white Maltese?"

"Uh-huh," I said with a nod.

"A chubby Maltese?" Miss O asked.

"Uh-huh!" I said again.

"Named Rocky?" Isabella asked.

I grinned. "How ever did you guess?" I asked with a laugh.

"I think it's perfect," Miss O said. "Harlie Rox and her little dog Fat Rocky! I'm lovin' it!"

"Lovin' it lots!" Isabella agreed.

"And my father has this cool wall projector that he uses for work," I told the girls. "We can use it to project whatever Miss O draws right onto the wall, as large as we want it to be. Then all we have to do is trace it and paint it in. And presto—we'll have a life-size wall mural!"

"Sounds like a plan," Miss O said. Then she got all serious. "But I have a super-important question about tonight. Something I desperately need to know before I can agree to help you with this mural."

I narrowed my eyes and leaned in closer to hear the question. Isabella and Justine leaned in, too. "What is it, Miss O?" I asked.

Miss O quickly gazed around to see if anybody was listening. I couldn't, for the life of me, guess what was so super-serious.

"Okay. Here's what I need to know. What," she asked, "is your mother making for dinner?"

I hesitated for second, then burst out laughing. So did the others.

"You won't be disappointed," I assured her with a grin.

"Is it . . . ?"

I began to nod. "Yup!" I said with a knowing smile. "Mom's Famous Moo Shoo!"

Miss O clasped her hands together excitedly. "Awesome!" she exclaimed.

Yeah, it was awesome. Mom's Famous Moo Shoo was a family recipe handed down in our family for generations. It can be made with chicken or pork—but since I'm a vegetarian my mom makes a special moo shoo vegetable just for me! It's sooo good! So good, in fact, that once I started thinking about it, I could hardly think about anything else for the rest of the afternoon!

Chapter 4
Harlie Rox

I had the most amazing idea for Harlie Rox, three minutes before the bell rang at the end of the day. Problem was, I couldn't tell anybody because class was still going on.

What if, I thought, Harlie Rox had an electric guitar with her at all times, and she could use it to ward off bad guys by playing extra-loud chords? The chords could be so super-incredibly loud, that their decibel levels could shatter the eardrums of criminals!

I couldn't wait to tell Miss O. I had an idea of what I wanted the guitar to look like: Black, with hot pink Chinese characters that meant peace and rock 'n' roll.

When the bell finally rang, I grabbed my book bag and raced outside and onto the bus.

"Hey! Whoa, Harlie!" said my bus driver, Perri. "What's the rush?" Perri was Asian-American, like me, and she had two teenage sons who both played the electric guitar.

"Hi, Perri!" I said. "I just can't wait to tell my friends about my idea for this superhero I'm creating."

As I told Perri about Harlie Rox, Miss O hopped up the bus steps and handed Perri her note from the office.

"You're going to Harlie's today?" Perri asked as she read the note.

"Yes," Miss O replied.

"Sounds fun!" Perri said.

As we walked down the aisle to find seats, I started telling Miss O my ideas.

"Wow! What a great idea!" she said about the black and pink guitar.

"Right? And don't you think it'd be so cool if we make Fat Rocky have a little electric guitar, too? Maybe he could always wear it on his back or something?" I suggested.

"Hmmm. What if we just gave Rocky a bandana to wear around his neck that matched Harlie Rox's guitar? Because I don't think a dog can actually hold a guitar."

"Good point," I agreed. That's why it was so great Miss O was helping me with Harlie Rox. Not only was she an excellent artist, she was good at thinking stuff through, too.

As we sat down and talked more about Harlie Rox and Fat Rocky, Justine arrived, and a minute later Isabella and Juliette showed up, too. We filled them in on our plans for the guitar and the bandana.

"Oh, and you have to make a guitar pick necklace and earrings for

Harlie Rox!" Juliette said. Like the ones you always wear, Harlie," she pointed out.

I put my hand up to touch my favorite necklace. I'd made it out of super-cool, multicolored guitar picks I bought on Canal Street in New York City on a shopping trip with my dad. My father helped me burn holes through the picks to make them into jewelry. The necklace was my favorite, and I wore it all the time, except when I did gymnastics.

"Oh! And I have an idea!" Isabella chimed in. "What if we put an 'HR' on the guitar pick necklace for Harlie Rox? Like Superman wears an 'S' on his chest and Batman wears a bat?"

I pictured how cool that would look. "Genius idea!" I told Isabella. "I really love it!"

"Me, too," Miss O said. "Oooh! I can't wait to get started! After this is finished, can you all help me do a mural in my room, too?"

"And mine!" Justine piped in.

Miss O and I were discussing possible superhero outfits for Harlie Rox when there was a tap on my shoulder. I glanced up to see Lanie, with the saddest expression ever, and her eyes filled with tears.

"Didn't you save me a seat?" she asked.

I bit my lower lip. I'd completely forgotten I'd promised to save her a seat! I quickly gazed around to see if there was an empty seat anywhere. Luckily, Justine wasn't sitting with anybody. Great!

"Here, Lanie!" I said. "Justine has room for you!"

Lanie stood in the aisle and didn't budge.

"It's okay, Lanie," I told her. "Justine is one of my very best friends!"

"But I want to sit with you," Lanie whined. "You said you would save me a seat!"

Miss O quickly jumped up. "No problem, Lanie!" she said. "I need to sit with Justine anyway, so why don't you sit here and I'll sit with Justine?"

I smiled at Miss O. That was nice of her to offer. I know she was really getting into discussing Harlie Rox with me, and it would have been great for us to sit together for the ride home and keep talking about it.

Lanie's expression instantly changed. "Great!" she said.

I moved over to the window and made room for the kindergartener.

"So, how was your first day, Lanie?" I asked.

A second later, I wished I hadn't!

Lanie talked on and on about her first day of school. And Holy Moley, this kid could talk! She went on and on about her new teacher, the kids in her class, the job chart they had in the classroom, and about how she got to be line leader that day.

I smiled politely and nodded every so often so Lanie would know I was listening. Meanwhile, I could see my friends were deep into discussion about other, important stuff, and I was so jealous!

"So then you know what happened?" Lanie asked me.

I shook my head. Actually, I hadn't been paying attention to what she was saying, so I had no idea what she was talking about.

"Mrs. Biscari let me write on the blackboard!" she proudly declared.

"Uh-huh. Great. That's great, Lanie," I said.

"Harlie?"

I sighed. There was more. "Yeah?"

"How come school buses are always yellow?"

I gazed out the bus window. Then I groaned, realizing the bus hadn't even left the school yet.

It was going to be another very long bus trip.

My friends and I arranged the beanbag chairs in my Latte Lounge so we were all facing each other. As usual, Rocky lay down in the middle of our circle, perking up his ears every so often when someone bent over to pet him. We sipped our decaf mocha lattes and listened to music.

"I love the Latte Lounge!" Juliette sighed as she sipped.

Isabella popped a cookie in her mouth. "Me, too," she said. "Even though I don't drink lattes. This is the coolest room!" She took a sip of chocolate milk and snuggled deeper into her beanbag.

"Just wait until we finish the mural," Miss O said. "This room is gonna rock!"

I looked at the drawings of Harlie Rox and Fat Rocky that Miss O and I had just finished. They had come out great.

Justine made a suggestion about having Harlie Rox's costume match the guitar. So Miss O had changed the guitar to hot pink with black Chinese characters, and made Harlie Rox's costume black with hot pink Chinese characters. It looked sooooo cool! Now all we had to do was trace the image onto a clear plastic sheet and put the sheet into the projector. The projector would project a much, much bigger image onto the wall, and then we could trace over that image, right onto the wall. The last step would be painting it in, which we could all help do.

After our latte break, Isabella and Juliette made lists of what we would need from the paint store. My dad had promised he would take me there over the weekend to get everything I needed for painting. Justine was helping, too, taking lots of pictures while also helping us move things around to make room for the mural.

We were having so much fun, dancing around the room while we worked, that I didn't even hear the knocking at first.

Juliette heard something and flipped off the iPod SoundDock. "I think someone is at your door," she said.

We listened in silence for another second, then heard the knocking, too. The girls followed me to the door and I pulled it open. To my surprise it was Mrs. Kappel and Lanie.

"Hello, hello, hello!" Mrs. Kappel said brightly. "I just had to come down and thank you for watching out for Lanie today!"

"Hi, Harlie!" Lanie said.

"Hey, Lanie," I replied. "You don't have to thank me, Mrs. Kappel," I added. "It was no big deal."

"Well, thank you anyway!" she said. "Lanie said you were so nice to her. I really appreciate it!"

"What are you doing?" Lanie asked.

"Oh, my friends and I are working on a project," I explained. "We're painting a mural in the Latte, er, in the spare room."

"Fun!" Lanie cried. Then she turned to her mother. "Can I stay, Mom? Can I?"

My eyes widened. Oh, no!

"Well, sweetheart, I don't know. Harlie is busy with her friends right now."

Yes! I said in my head. Very busy! Very busy with friends!

"Oh, please, Mom? Just for a little while? Can't I? Please?"

Mrs. Kappel looked at me. "Well, if it's okay with Harlie," she said, "it's okay with me. But just until dinner."

Lanie looked at me with pleading eyes. "Harlie?" she asked. "Can we have a playdate for a little while?"

I heard Juliette snicker. A playdate! Sheesh!

"Um, well, we were sort of—" I stopped myself when I saw Lanie's smile start to fade. "Um, sure, Lanie," I said. "You can come in for a while. But just until dinner like your mom said."

Lanie raced inside so quickly, I was pretty sure she'd already forgotten her mom had been standing in the doorway.

"I'll bring her up before dinner, Mrs. Kappel," I promised.

"Oh, you're an absolute angel!" Mrs. Kappel said. "An angel, angel, angel!"

I closed the door and headed back to the Latte Lounge to find Lanie already nestled in a beanbag, petting Rocky, and asking questions.

"What's your doggie's name?" she asked

"His name is Rocky," I told her.

"How come?"

"Well, his real name is Rocket, but I call him Rocky."

"Why?" she asked.

I looked pleadingly at my friends for help.

"Hey, do you have any pets, Lanie?" Miss O asked.

"Just a goldfish," Lanie replied. "Her name is Lovey." Then Lanie pointed to my amplifier. "What's that?" she asked.

"Harlie's amplifier," Isabella told her.

"What's it for?"

"Her electric guitar," Miss O replied.

"How does it work?"

I sighed. "It gets hooked up to the electric guitar and that's where the sound comes out," I explained.

"Can I hear you play?" Lanie asked.

"Well, I guess I can—" I started.

But before I could finish, Lanie was already looking at something else. "What are those?" she asked pointing over to my comic book collection.

I panicked as Lanie took a step toward my priceless books. "Lanie! Don't touch those!" I yelled at her from across the room.

Lanie stopped dead in her tracks. Slowly she faced me and I could see the look of panic on her face. Everyone else was looking at me in disbelief. I guess I had yelled at her pretty loudly.

"Wait. I'm sorry, Lanie," I said. "I didn't mean to yell like that. It's just that I'm very protective of my comic books. They are very valuable. And I try to keep them in mint condition."

Lanie stood there quietly. I wasn't sure if she was going to ask to go home, or burst into tears. I felt terrible!

"Lanie, really. I'm sorry for yelling. I know you wouldn't ruin the comic books or anything. I'm just . . . really sorry."

It was drop-dead quiet in the room and Miss O and the others were still staring at me. I think we were all wondering the same thing. Was Lanie going to tell her mother I had yelled at her?

"Harlie?" Lanie asked, breaking the silence.

"Yes?" I replied with a gulp.

"What's mint condition?" she asked.

Same old Lanie.

I took a deep breath, then exhaled in relief. Okay, we had avoided a possible catastrophe. "Mint condition," I explained, "is what comic book collectors call books that are in perfect condition with no crinkles or ripped pages."

"Why?"

Oh, brother.

"Listen," I said, changing the subject, "Why don't I go check on the moo shoo."

"Moo shoo?" Lanie asked.

Isabella took over the question-answering job to give me a break. "Moo shoo is a Chinese dish that Harlie's mother makes. It rocks! It's her best dish ever!" she explained to Lanie.

"Is it from a cow?" Lanie asked.

"Huh?" Isabella uttered looking confused.

"You know, moo?" Lanie asked.

We all laughed.

"No, it's sort of like a burrito," Juliette explained, "but it's Chinese food."

"Why do they call it moo shoo?" Lanie asked.

Juliette looked at me helplessly.

"No one knows" I said quickly. "It's a mystery!"

"But it's really delish!" Miss O went on. "You get these pancake thingies, and you lay them out flat. Then you put the vegetables on top with some sauce and then you roll it up!"

"But why is it called moo shoo?" Lanie demanded.

"I'll go ask my mom," I told them all, "and see how it's coming along. It's practically dinnertime anyway."

"Yeah, I'm starved," Miss O commented.

"Me, too!" the others replied.

I left the Latte Lounge and closed the door behind me. Honestly, that kid was high-maintenance! But I was still feeling pretty badly about yelling at her. Why had I had such a cow? She'd only been walking over to see my comics. It wasn't as if she were going to throw them around the room and then jump all over them.

I decided maybe the reason I'd gotten so bent out of shape was that I just wasn't great around little kids. Because I didn't have any younger brothers or sisters I wasn't used to having them around. I mean, it wasn't that I didn't like little kids or anything. I just didn't enjoy hanging out with them. We had nothing in common, after all.

Anyway, I was thinking about this as I headed down the apartment hallway toward the kitchen. But as I walked, I realized something else was wrong.

I didn't smell anything cooking.

That was weird because usually, when my mother makes moo shoo, the whole house smells great. Now? Nothing. Not even an onion sautéing or anything.

"Mom?" I asked, poking my head in the kitchen.

To my surprise, the kitchen was empty! The lights were off, and so was the stove. Nothing was cooking, frying, or sautéing. Mom wasn't chopping veggies or even mixing up her special moo shoo sauce.

"Mom?" I called out in a panic. "Where are you? What's going on?"

She wasn't in the living room, the dining room, or her bedroom, and I checked the laundry area and she wasn't there either. Something was definitely wrong! Where could she be? When I had gotten home from school with the girls, I'd kissed her hello, then headed for the Latte Lounge. Mom had said she was going to start the moo shoo. A big celebratory moo shoo dinner to celebrate the fact that I'd made the gymnastics team.

When I walked past my parents' bedroom a second time, something caught my eye. Mom hadn't answered me when I called for her a few minutes ago, but when I peered into her bedroom for a second look, I suddenly realized why.

She was fast asleep in her bed!

"Mom!" I said, shaking her shoulder. "Mom! Wake up!"

My mother bolted up from the pillow. "Harlie?" she said groggily. "What? What's the matter? Was I sleeping?"

"Yes, Mom! You were out cold!"

My mother yawned and stretched her arms over her head. "Boy, I was so tired," she mumbled. "I don't know what's gotten into me lately."

"Mom!" I cried. Obviously, she'd forgotten about dinner and the girls.

"What is it, Harlie?" she said, looking at me strangely.

"The moo shoo!" I replied.

Mom gasped. "Oh, no!" she said. "Harlie, I'm so sorry! I . . . I . . . fell asleep!"

My shoulders slumped. "Does that mean you can't make the moo shoo tonight?" I asked.

Mom checked the clock by her bed. "I'm afraid not, sweetie," she said. "There's no time."

"Aw, Mom!"

"How about we order pizza?" she offered.

I sighed disappointedly. "Yeah, okay," I muttered.

"Sorry, hon," Mom apologized again as she rubbed the sleep from her eyes.

I headed for the door. "Whatever," I muttered.

But as I walked down the hallway, back to my friends, I have to tell you I was mad. And then I felt guilty for feeling mad! But I had really been looking forward to the moo shoo! We had all been.

How could my mom have forgotten about the celebration dinner like that?

Chapter 5
Mini Me

The following Monday morning, my alarm went off at five a.m. as usual. But today, even though Miss O's and Juliette's voices were as silly as ever . . . :

> Like, totally!
> Like, wow!
> Like, get outta bed right now! . . .

. . . I was in a pretty crummy mood. I snapped off the alarm before they even finished and I dragged myself out of bed.

It had been a whole week since I'd learned about coming in first in my level at the Flips Club. And four days since I'd performed my floor exercise for the Team USA Classic judges. And I'd spent five whole days riding the bus to and from school with Lanie, and answering all twelve billion of her questions. But even all those things combined weren't the reason I was feeling crummy.

Mostly, I was feeling crummy because of my mother.

For as long as I can remember, my mother and I have been really close. We share secrets and jokes, and we just like being together. But lately, our relationship has changed. Mom was acting strange. How? Well, I can't explain it exactly. Just trust me—she was different.

Like when she overslept last week and made me late for gymnastics. And when she fell asleep that time and forgot to make the big moo shoo dinner. Then there was this past Thursday, when she'd completely forgotten to pick me up after school! There I was, standing in front of the building for so long, my fingers had gone numb from the cold. The buses had long gone, and she was nowhere to be seen.

That afternoon, we had made plans to go to our favorite gymnastics shop in Westchester to buy a brand-new outfit for the big floor routine for the judges. But after an hour had passed, I knew she'd forgotten. I went inside to call her but couldn't reach her on her cell or at home. So I had to call and ask Miss O's mother to come pick me up—it was so embarrassing! As it turned out, when I finally found Mom, she was at Starbucks with a friend and had completely lost track of time.

I even asked Dad if he knew why she was acting so weird lately. But he thought I was just imagining things, that it was all just a bunch of coincidences, and that Mom was still Mom, only a little overwhelmed with work.

Whatever. We would see.

Mom had invited the girls over again tonight for moo shoo dinner—

to make up for forgetting last week. She knew we were all looking forward to it again, so if anything happened to ruin the plans this time, I'd know something was up for sure!

After I finished washing up, I pulled open my dresser drawer to get a clean unitard for practice. But I couldn't find one.

"Mom?" I called out. "Are there any unitards in the dryer?"

Mom didn't answer, so I went to check for myself. I peered into the dryer only to find it empty. In the washing machine, however, were all my unitards. They were still wet.

I groaned, pulled out the wet clothes and stuffed them into the dryer. Then I turned the dryer on and stomped down the hallway to the kitchen. No way would they be ready in time for practice.

"Mom! I don't have any clean unitards!" I called out. "Mom?"

The kitchen was dark. No one was inside—and worse, no coffee was percolating. I headed for my parents bedroom, where I could hear the shower running.

"Mom?"

To my surprise, it was Dad in the shower and not Mom. She was still in bed!

"Mom!" I cried.

My mother bolted upright. "What? Oh, Harlie! Is it five?"

"Yes! I mean, it's ten to six! We have to leave!"

My mother leapt up from her bed and began getting dressed as fast as she could.

"Didn't Dad wake you?" I asked her.

"Yes, I think he did," she said with a yawn. "But I must have fallen back asleep. Don't worry, I'll be ready!"

"It's just that I don't have any clean unitards," I told her.

My mother groaned. "None in the dryer?" she asked sleepily.

I shook my head. "Nope. In the wash."

Mom sighed. "I guess I forgot to dry them last night. Sorry. Uh, can you wear something else?" she asked.

"Yeah, I guess," I said. But my mother knew as well as I did that Coach Ilana prefers that we wear unitards for practice.

In my room, I found an old pair of biker shorts and a tank top and got dressed as quickly as possible. Unfortunately, it wasn't quickly enough, and Mom and I left late anyway. When we got to the gym, we were five minutes late for practice. Coach Ilana did not look happy.

"This is the third time you're late," she said to me.

"I know. I'm very sorry, coach," I said.

"Harlie, do you want to qualify for the Classic or not?" she asked.

I stopped my warming up exercises to look at her. "Yes, I do!" I said.

"Because there are many, many girls who dream of competing in the Classic," Coach Ilana continued. "If you are not sure about continuing, please let me know now and I will give the spot to someone else."

I felt my heart sink into my stomach. "No! Please don't! I really want to do this!" I insisted. "I promise, I won't be late again. Even if I have to wake up earlier!"

Coach Ilana nodded. "Okay, then. Let's get started."

I finished warming up, then headed over to the high bar to practice a little. I chalked my hands, then jumped up to catch the bar. I gave a little swing and pulled my body up and over the bar. I flipped completely around twice, then flew into a perfect dismount, landing with my arms in a flawless, dramatic mid-air position.

That was actually pretty good, I thought to myself, hoping Coach Ilana had seen it.

Happily, I noticed she had. She nodded at me and gave me a thumbs-up. Whew! I was glad. I simply had to do whatever I could to convince her that I was committed to doing my best.

Still in my dismount position, I gave a quick glance over to the viewing stands to see if my mother had caught my impressive moves, too. I spotted her, just as she was leaping up from her seat to run out the door!

Huh?

I put my arms down and went after her. "Mom?" I called out. "What's wrong?"

I raced across the gym and pushed through the doors she had just gone through. They led to a waiting room, but she wasn't there. Anxiously, I flew down the hall to the coffee bar in the gym lobby, but she wasn't there either. Then I headed for the ladies' room.

"Mom?" I called out, sticking my head inside the bathroom.

I heard someone clear their throat. "Harlie, I'm in here."

I stepped inside to find my mother leaning over the sink, splashing water on her face.

"Mom, what's going on?" I asked. "Are you sick?"

"I just really don't feel well," my mom said as she reached for a paper towel to dry her face. I caught her reflection in the mirror as she stood up and she looked just awful!

"I think I'm going to have to cancel dinner," she said glumly.

Later that morning, as I stood in front of the building waiting for the bus, Steve the doorman knew immediately that something was wrong.

"Are you nervous about not having heard from the judges yet?" he asked me.

"Kind of," I told him. "I mean, I'm definitely anxious about that. I want to go to the Classic so badly! It's, like, the most important thing in the world right now!"

Steve nodded. He's known me ever since I started competing in gymnastics when I was four years old. So he really knows how much gymnastics means to me.

"It's a lot of things," I told him. "My life is very complicated right now."

Steve nodded again. "You're a very busy young lady," he said. "And when you're into doing so many wonderful things, life sometimes gets in the way."

Just then, Steve leaned in to open the door. Mrs. Kappel and Lanie stepped out, into the brisk air. I noticed immediately that something about Lanie looked different.

But what was it?

Lanie raced up to me. "Hi, Harlie!" she said. "Look!" she twirled around for me to see her new jacket and jeans. And boots!

Oh my god! She was dressed exactly like me! She was Mini Me! Right down to the rolled up jeans!

"Do you like it?" she asked. "I got the same book bag as you, too!"

I had to grin. She did look pretty cute. Plus, she was probably the coolest kindergartener at the moment! I just wasn't sure how I felt about having a clone of myself walking around Sage.

"Yeah, I like it, Lanie," I said.

"She insisted on rolling up her pants, just like you do!" Mrs. Kappel gushed. "Doesn't she look so, so, so cute?"

"Very," I said, wondering where Mrs. Kappel had found high-top boots like mine in such a tiny size.

"Harlie?" Mrs. Kappel asked, her voice all serious-like. "Can I talk to you about something?"

"Sure, Mrs. Kappel. What is it?"

"As you know, I work at home for my job as an interior designer," she said.

I nodded. Mrs. Kappel was a well-known interior designer. Lanie had told me all about her mother during one of our long bus trips. Lanie had said that her mother designed a famous restaurant in New York City and a few movie stars' apartments.

"Well, now that Lanie is in kindergarten and we don't have a nanny anymore, I've been finding it hard to work after she gets home from school."

"Uh-huh," I said, peering down Broadway to see if the bus was on its way.

"I was going to hire a nanny for an hour every day, to pick Lanie up from the bus and watch her until I can finish my work, but then I had an idea. I wondered if I could hire you?"

Me?

"Me?" I asked. "Babysit?"

"Yes!" Mrs. Kappel gushed. "Lanie simply adores you, and it would just be for an hour every day. I would be home the whole time, just in my office working."

"I don't know, Mrs. Kappel. I don't think I'm babysitting material," I said, remembering how I'd yelled at Lanie just last week for merely walking near my comic books.

"Oh, don't be silly!" Mrs. Kappel insisted. "You are fab, fab, fab with my Lanie!"

I shifted on my feet, wondering how I was going to say no and not have the Kappels think of me as a witch who hated children. Then I had an idea . . .

"See, I'm very busy with gymnastics and—"

"I would pay you, too," Mrs. Kappel went on, ignoring me. "Five dollars a day. That would be twenty-five dollars each week."

I swallowed hard. Twenty-five dollars a week? Wow! That could buy a lot of comic books!

"Wow, Mrs. Kappel. That would be very generous," I said.

"Nonsense!" she insisted. "You would be helping me a great deal. So is it a yes?"

I looked down at Lanie, er, Mini Me, and her eyes were wide with excitement. She was even nodding a little, as if she were begging me to say yes!

Twenty-five bucks a week was a lot of money, I thought, trying hard not to think about Lanie's constant chatting and endless questions. How bad could it be to deal with her for just a measly ol' hour a day? I wondered.

"It's a yes," I said, just as the school bus pulled up.

Mrs. Kappel clasped her hands together. "I am so glad!" she said. Then she pulled twenty-five dollars from her coat pocket and thrust it into my hands. "Here's your first week's pay!" she added. She kissed Lanie on the cheek and waved as we climbed up to the bus together. As Lanie and I took our seat, we looked out the window to see Mrs. Kappel still waving. In my hand, I could still feel the crisp five-dollar bills she had given me.

This was going to be the easiest money I ever made!

"Harlie?" Lanie asked as the bus pulled away. "Can you count to a googol?"

I looked at her. "What?"

"I said, can you count to a googol? I can! Watch! One, two, three, four . . ."

Chapter 6
The Day
Everything Changed

I had been getting pretty used to my routine lately—riding the bus to school with Lanie in the mornings, racing to her classroom and dropping her off, then racing back over to the "doorz" to meet the girls. Today, I couldn't wait to get to the "doorz" and show them my five five-dollar bills and tell them about my new job!

When I got there, I waved the cash out in front of me.

"Hmmmm, let's see!" I said dramatically. "How much is here? Five, ten, fifteen . . ."

"Hey! Where'd you get all that money?" Miss O asked.

I smiled at my friends. "I have a job now!" I exclaimed.

The girls all looked at me. "A job? Doing what?" Justine asked.

"Babysitting!" I replied.

"Babysitting?" Miss O asked.

"Babysitting?" Justine repeated.

"But I thought you hated kids?" Isabella commented.

I sighed. "No, I don't hate them. I just don't care for them that much."

Miss O laughed. "Then why the babysitting job, Harlie?" she asked.

"Because Lanie's mom is going to pay me five dollars a day to watch Lanie for just one hour a day after school!"

"Get out!" Miss O said. "I would love a job like that. Sounds like a cinch."

"Yeah, really, Harlie," Isabella said. "You're going to be rolling in dough."

I smiled and shoved the money in my jacket pocket. "You said it!" I exclaimed.

Miss O picked up her book bag and slung it over her shoulder. "Okay, congratulations on your new job, Harlie," she said. "I'm just thinking maybe you ought to ask Lanie's mother to pay you by the question!"

I giggled. "Good idea!"

"Glad I could be of help. But for now, I'd better get to class, or the Hinter Monster will have my head! Plus, I have to drop off my permission slip at the office."

My eyes narrowed. "Permission slip?" I asked. "For what?"

Miss O snickered. "Du-uh? For getting off the bus at your house after school today? Remember?"

I stared at her blankly.

"Harlie Rox? Moo shoo?" she added.

I covered my face with my hands. I'd completely forgotten about our afternoon plans! I'd been so excited about my new job (okay, stoked more about my new salary) that I'd forgotten the girls were all coming over!

"Don't kill me, guys," I said meekly. "But my job starts today. And I think my mother might be too sick to make dinner."

Miss O sighed. "You mean this afternoon?" she said.

I nodded. "I'm sorry!"

Justine groaned. "But we were really looking forward to the moo shoo," she said.

"And to helping finish up the mural," Isabella added.

I thought for a moment.

"Wait!" I said. "We can still keep our plans. If you don't mind having Lanie hang around with us for a little while. I bet Mrs. Kappel won't mind if I babysit for Lanie at my apartment. That is, if you guys don't mind."

Justine shrugged. "I don't mind," she said.

"Me neither," Miss O added.

"Or me," Isabella chimed in.

I breathed a sigh of relief. "Thanks, guys! You totally rock!"

"Yeah, we know!" Miss O exclaimed.

As I walked to class, I was happy I'd thought of a way to watch Lanie and keep my plans. I didn't want to disappoint my buds, plus, I'd really been looking forward to working on the mural and all. Anyway, I was glad they had been so understanding. And I was sure Mrs. Kappel would be under-standing, too.

The only person I wasn't so sure about was Lanie.

Luckily, my mother had made a miraculous recovery! In fact, she was already shredding carrots by the time we got off the bus. And luckily, Mrs. Kappel was more than happy to let me watch Lanie at my house.

This time, we left the door to the Latte Lounge open so we could smell the moo shoo cooking. (I wasn't taking any chances.) And boy, did it smell good! The whole apartment smelled like my favorite restaurant in Chinatown. Miss O kept running into the kitchen to give us reports on which step my mother was up to with her recipe. (If I haven't mentioned it before, Miss O loves to cook and bake. Actually, she's obsessed with it. And she's very good at it, too.)

As for the mural, I hate to say that things weren't moving along as quickly as I had hoped. With Miss O's running back and forth from the kitchen to the Latte Lounge, the actual painting of the mural was going very slowly. Juliette and Isabella were doing a lot of the work, and Justine was helping out by mixing colors and washing paintbrushes, but we would be getting a lot more done if I had been able to help, too.

And why couldn't I help? Because for most of the first hour the girls were painting, I was sitting on the floor listening to Lanie describe every last one of her Polly Pocket dolls.

And all their accessories.

"See, Harlie? This Polly Pocket comes with her own laptop computer. And it has a teeny-tiny computer case, and an itty-bitty cell phone! Isn't that so cool?"

"Yeah. Cool," I mumbled.

Truth? I had never been so bored before in all my life. I wasn't the biggest doll fan to begin with, but I really disliked dolls that were so small you could barely find their shoes when you dropped one on the carpet. (Which I had just done.)

"You don't like my Polly Pockets, do you?" Lanie asked me as I secretly dug around for the dropped shoe.

I decided I would tell Lanie the truth. "Actually, no. I don't like Polly Pockets," I told her. "I don't really like playing with dolls in general. But we can keep playing with them if you want. I don't mind that much."

Suddenly, Lanie got angry. "Well, I like them!" she snapped at me. "I know you just want to play with your friends instead of me!" she added.

"Well, yes! I kind of do!" I said, feeling a little irritated at her for being so snappy.

Isabella shot me a look.

"What?" I asked her.

She pointed to Lanie, who indeed looked miserable.

I softened a little. "I didn't mean that I didn't want to play with you, too,

Lanie," I said gently. "I'd just like to do something else. With all of you. Why can't we find something we all like to do?"

Lanie shrugged. "Like gymnastics?" she asked.

"Well, I like gymnastics, but none of my friends do gymnastics."

"I like to do gymnastics," Lanie said. "I can do a cartwheel, you know."

"Yeah?" I asked. "Come show me," I said.

Lanie forgot all about pouting and sprung up from the floor. She followed me into the living room where the carpet was nice and soft. I opened the little gymnastics mat my uncle had given me for my seventh birthday.

"Go ahead," I said. "Show me what you can do."

Lanie stood at the edge of the mat, then did an almost perfect cartwheel. I was impressed!

"That was pretty good, Lanie!" I said.

"Yeah, you're really good at that," Miss O agreed, as she passed us on her way from the kitchen to the Latte Lounge.

"Let me teach you a trick," I told Lanie. "It will make every cartwheel you do for the rest of your life perfect!"

Lanie's eyes widened. "Really? Okay!"

I showed Lanie the special way I hold my right hand before going into a cartwheel. And wouldn't you know it, ten minutes later, she had it down pat! She really was a smart kid. And a fast learner. It kind of made me proud, too, that I'd taught her that.

"Thanks, Harlie! This is great! I can't wait to show my mom! And my friend Ally!"

I grinned, then remembered the time. "Okay, speaking of your mom, I told her I'd have you home by now. So let's get your Polly Pockets and head up to your apartment."

Lanie frowned. "Can't I play with you a little longer?" she asked.

"Not today," I told her.

"Why not?" she asked.

I sighed. This kid was relentless.

"Lanie, we'll have lots of time to play again and do gymnastics together," I explained. "But my friends came over today to do stuff with me. It wouldn't be nice if I ignored them."

"But can't I at least have moop shoop with you guys?" she asked.

I tried not to laugh out loud. "It's moo shoo. Not moop shoop," I said. "And not tonight. Maybe another time."

That's when sweet little Lanie—for whom I was now in charge of every day for one hour after school—stomped her sweet little foot at me. Even Rocky was surprised by the loud stomp and he got up with a jolt and left the room.

"No!" Lanie said.

"Huh?" I asked.

"I said, 'No.' I don't want to go home!"

Miss O, who had seen the entire thing, looked at me with wide open eyes. I think neither of us knew what to do.

"But you have to, Lanie," I said. "You can't stay here any longer."

Lanie just shook her head. "I'm not going home," she insisted.

Juliette, Justine, and Isabella came out of the Latte Lounge to see what was going on.

"Lanie won't go home," I told them.

"Why not?" Justine asked.

"Because I don't want to yet," Lanie declared. "I'm not finished playing!"

"And she stomped her foot at me," I told them.

"Really?" Isabella asked.

I nodded. Then we all just stood there for a bit longer, not knowing how to handle the mini tantrum Lanie was having in front of us.

To tell you the truth, I knew how I would have liked to handle it. I would have liked to throw her and her dumb Polly Pockets over my shoulder and toss 'em all in the elevator and send 'em upstairs. Lanie was really acting like a brat!

Why had I taken this job? I wondered glumly.

Then I remembered: For the twenty-five bucks a week. That was why.

"Come on, Lanie," I said, more sternly than before. "We're going!"

"No!" she shouted at me. "No, no, no, no, no!" With each "No!" she gave another loud stomp. I was sure Rocky was hiding under my bed in the other room.

"You're being a baby, Lanie," I told her.

"I'm not a baby!" she yelled. "You are!"

"Cut it out, Lanie, and just come with me!" I said in exasperation.

"I said I don't want to!" Lanie insisted.

"Then I'm going to call your mother!" I threatened her.

"I don't care!" she shot back. "I'm not going home! I'm staying here and having moop shoop with you guys!"

"No, you're not!" I said angrily.

"Yes, I am!"

"Are not!"

"Am, too!"

"Are not!"

"Am, too!"

I felt my blood boiling. And my hands were clenched together so hard that I could feel my fingers throbbing.

"Lanie, you're really making me mad!"

"I don't care!" she shouted at me. "I'm mad at you, too!"

Was this really worth it? I wondered. Was twenty-five bucks really worth this? At the moment, I didn't think so.

I took a deep breath and leaned in really close to Lanie. "Look, Lanie," I breathed, trying to keep my calm. "The playdate is over. We are leaving right now!" I stared at her, giving her my most threatening evil villain stare.

But Lanie didn't respond. She just stood firmly with her arms folded across her chest in defiance. And I think she was giving me her most threatening evil villain stare.

"Okay, how about this?" I said, offering up one last suggestion before I really blew my cool. "If you come upstairs with me right now, I'll make sure it's just me and you for the rest of the week."

That got her attention.

Lanie glanced up at me. "Really?" she asked. "Just me and you?"

I nodded. "Really. Let's just go."

And as if by magic, Lanie smiled brightly.

"Okay!" she said. It was as if everything was just super-peachy-keen and she hadn't just been possessed by aliens. "You're the best, Harlie!"

My friends all watched in utter amazement as Lanie picked up her Polly Pockets case and skipped behind me toward the door.

"G'bye, everyone!" she called out cheerfully.

"Bye, Lanie," they called back, still sounding stunned by Lanie's total transformation.

"Harlie?" Lanie asked as we stepped into the elevator.

I took a deep breath and exhaled loudly.

"What, Lanie?" I asked in exasperation.

"How do elevators work?"

I shook my head as I pressed the button for Lanie's floor. I knew she lived on the sixth floor, but at the moment, I was sure this little girl standing next to me, holding her Polly Pocket playset and smiling as if everything in the world was just perfect, had to be from a place even further up than the sixth floor.

Like Mars, for example.

After a totally scrumptious dinner, my friends' parents arrived to take them all home. Despite all the drama with Lanie, we had really made a lot of progress on the mural. I made them all promise to come back and help me finish the job over the weekend and they'd all agreed.

The mural itself was really looking great. Harlie Rox was going to be one kickin' cool superhero! Miss O had added a bandana to Harlie Rox at the last minute, and spiked up her hair like a rock star. We had all agreed it looked way cool like that.

And Juliette was already working fast and furiously on a story idea for a Harlie Rox comic book. It was about a famous piece of artwork that gets stolen from MoMA and how Harlie Rox and Fat Rocky catch the thieves and save the day.

As for me, I was totally wiped out after my first day on the new job! So wiped I didn't even think I could finish my homework. (But I did.) When I'd finished it all, I changed into a sleep T-shirt and boxer shorts and vegged out in front of the TV with Rocky.

Vegging was really the perfect word for what I was doing. Not really listening to or concentrating on any program in particular, but just staring at the screen. I was rubbing my dog's fat belly and flipping channels, while one big question kept running through my mind.

Had I made a huge mistake in agreeing to babysit for Lanie?

For one thing, I wasn't sure I was cut out to be a babysitter. I've just never clicked with little kids. I wasn't used to hanging around them, and I sort of liked having things all to myself. Like my friends, and my free time—I guess I just don't really like sharing that much!

And another thing? Lanie could be a real brat sometimes! I mean, most of the time she was pretty okay and all. And sometimes, I even enjoyed hanging out with her. But then there were those other times—like tonight—when she was just awful!

So yeah, the extra money is cool and all. But I was starting to think it wasn't really worth having to suffer through Polly Pockets and tantrums. Or worth having to resort to bribery just to convince a five-year-old it was time to go home. I mean, what if I have to do that every single day from now on?

These were the things that I was thinking about when my parents came into the living room and sat down on both sides of me on the sofa: That I was through dealing with whiney little kids. And that tomorrow I would tell Mrs. Kappel that the deal was off.

Babysitting Harlie was a thing of the past.

I was about to clue my parents in on my decision when my father reached for the remote control.

"You can change it," I told him. "I'm not really watching anything."

Instead, he turned the TV off.

"Harlie?" he said. "Your mom and I need to talk to you."

As I straightened up on the sofa, I glanced at them curiously. They both seemed kind of anxious about something.

"What's up?" I asked.

My parents exchanged looks and I suddenly had a weird feeling in the pit of my stomach. Why were they acting so weird?

"Uh, what's going on?" I asked again. "You guys seem weird." Then a horrible thought occurred to me. "Are we moving?" I asked in a panic.

My father laughed. "No, honey! We're not moving."

I leaned back against the sofa cushions. "Whew!" I said. "Because I don't want to move."

"Neither do we," my mother said.

"Still, we are about to go through some big changes around here," Dad said. "All of us."

Huh?

What was he talking about? What big changes?

Did he get a new job? Did Mom?

"Harlie," Dad went on, "your mom and I love you so much."

The pit in my stomach grew larger.

Was he about to tell me they were getting a divorce? "Your Mom and I love you so much . . .'" That sounded just like what people getting divorced say to their kids!

I jumped up from the sofa. "Dad! I know that! I know you do! Please tell me what's going on?"

It was my mother who cut to the chase.

"Harlie, the reason I threw up this morning at the gym is because I'm pregnant," she blurted out.

I froze. I couldn't think of anything to say.

Pregnant?

"Isn't that great?" Dad cried. "We're having a baby!"

I still couldn't speak.

"A baby girl," Mom went on. "I'm pretty far along in my pregnancy," she added. "But I didn't know until today. I guess I've just been working so hard lately and—"

"You're pregnant?" I managed to say.

"Yes. I went to the doctor this morning and I took a test," my mother said.

"A baby girl?"

My mother nodded. For some reason, I suddenly thought about Lanie.

"Isn't it wonderful?" Dad said cheerfully.

I nodded, but all I could picture in my head was a little girl who could stomp her feet and throw a tantrum. "Wonderful" wasn't exactly the first word that came to mind.

"Of course," my mom went on, "there'll be many changes we'll have to make for when the baby comes. Big changes and little changes."

Ew, and diaper changes, I thought to myself.

"What kind of changes?" I asked.

My parents exchanged glances.

"Well, honey, for one thing, new babies don't sleep through the night," my father told me. "They have to eat every few hours, so they wake up a couple of times a night."

"Well that stinks," I said. "I have to wake up early in the morning for gymnastics!"

Again, my parents exchanged looks.

"That's another thing, sweetheart," my mother began, "once the baby comes, we'll have to talk to Coach Ilana about changing your training times. I won't be able to bring you there in the morning."

I gasped. No way!

"But listen, Harlie, I promise I'm going to do my best to make sure our lives continue as normally as possible!"

Yeah, right. I thought. That baby is going to make my life as un-normal as possible!

"We'll still go to MoMA on weekends, Sugar Plum," my father offered. "Just me and you if you'd like."

"And of course we'll still take our weekend walks in Central Park," my mother went on. "And think of how fun it will be to take the new baby to Central Park! And to Chinatown on Sundays! And to Starbucks!"

When she said the part about Starbucks, I felt like crying. That was *our* thing! What we always did together, just the two of us. I didn't want a dumb baby coming along with us and ruining everything.

Then a thought occurred to me. Was I going to have to share my room with . . . a baby?

"Wait a sec!" I said. "Where's the new baby going to sleep?" I asked them.

Both my parents were quiet.

"For the first few weeks, she'll sleep in our room in a bassinette," my father explained.

"And after that?" I asked anxiously. I had a feeling I wasn't going to like the answer.

"Then we'll move her into the nursery," my mother replied.

"The nursery?" I asked.

"Well, that's one of those 'big' changes I was talking about, Harl," my father said. "I'm afraid you're going to have to give up your Latte Lounge for the baby."

"What?" I asked in alarm. "But that's my room! All my stuff is in there!"

"Harlie, your new sister is going to need a room of her own," my father said.

"But what about all my things? My comics and my guitar and my beanbags? I can't fit them in my room! What am I going to do with them?"

"We'll work it out, Harlie," my mother promised. "Maybe we'll build a closet in the living room or something."

"And my mural!" I cried out loud. "We've been working so hard on it! What about that?"

"I'm sorry, Harlie," my father said quietly.

I couldn't believe what was happening. Everything was changing, and there wasn't anything I could do about it. I felt completely helpless.

"But you said you would try to keep things normal!" I insisted. "How is making me give up my Latte Lounge and put all my favorite things in a closet normal?"

"Harlie, you're looking at this all wrong!" my mother said. "You're going to have a sister! Do you know what a remarkable thing that is? Do you know what a special relationship you two girls are going to have?"

Ha! All I could think about was the "special" day Lanie and I had had. Care Bear lunch boxes, a zillion "Whys," Polly Pockets, and tantrums.

Special?

Not!

"I have a terrific idea!" my mother suddenly announced. "You can help me decorate the nursery!"

You mean my Latte Lounge, I wanted to say.

"Come on, Harlie, it'll be fun! You can help me pick the color scheme and the furniture. And your friends can help, too, if you want! Then, by the time the baby comes during the second week in July—"

I started to phase out as my mother spoke about cribs and curtains and something called a "diaper genie." I started feeling sick to my stomach.

"Harlie," my father said. "We understand this is a big adjustment. And a lot to comprehend. Do you want to talk about your feelings?"

I stared at him and shook my head blankly.

I certainly didn't feel like talking about my feelings at the moment.

Mostly because they weren't all good feelings.

What would I say anyway? That I really didn't like little kids and I definitely didn't want one living in our house? I could never tell them that. Especially when they both looked so darn excited about the baby on the way.

The baby on the way.

Hold on a sec.

Stop the presses!

"Mom? When did you say the baby was coming?" I asked.

"Sometime during the second week in July," she replied.

Oh, PERFECT.

That was just GREAT.

My mother was going to be in the hospital having my new sister . . .

the same exact week as the Team USA Classic in Miami!

Chapter 7
Oh, Baby!

To: gOalgirl, jujuBEE, JUSTme713, IzzyBELLA
Time: 12:47 a.m.
CC:
Subject: BIGGEST NEWZ EVUH!!!!

Hey, Guys.
Pls log on tomorrow morning ASAP!
Have BIG news . . . need to CHAT online!
No gym practice tomorrow a.m.—I'll be on buddy list
at 7 a.m. SHARP!

Harlie.

At 6:55 a.m. the next morning, I went online, hoping the girls had all received my urgent e-mail message from last night. One by one, I heard their buddy sounds as they logged on. Isabella was last, probably because she doesn't have a computer in her room. I quickly opened a five-way buddy chat.

> **harliegirl95:** every1 here???
>
> **jujuBEE:** here! :)
>
> **JUSTme713:** HERE
>
> **IzzyBELLA:** i'm here, Harl. wassup???
>
> **gOalgirl:** we r all here, H. whats the BIG newz? I
> couldn't sleep all nite after ur email!!!!
>
> **harliegirl95:** so,so BIG, couldnt wait for DOORZ.
>
> **JUSTme713:** tell us already!!! :O
>
> **harliegirl95:** ok. R u ready? Cuz this is big stuff!
>
> **gOalgirl:** is it about MIAMI???? did u QUALIFY???
>
> **jujuBEE:** did u?
>
> **harliegirl95:** not about Miami. ok, here it goes. I
> am going to have a baby sister!!!!!!!!!!!!!!

I waited for a second, but no one replied.

> **harliegirl95:** HEY, guys! Did u hear me? My mom is
> having a BABY! :O :O :O
>
> **gOalgirl:** OMG, H! That's UNBELIEVABLE! U R SOOO LUCKY!
>
> **JUSTme713:** I luv babies! That is so cool!

IzzyBELLA: harlie, that is Xellent newz! Can I hold
her? Can I help u babysit???

harliegirl95: a little early for that, izzy.

jujuBEE: I wish i had a little sister . . .

gOalgirl: HEY!!!! :(

jujuBEE: LOL! jk, MISSO! H, that is such awesome
news. R u stoked?? :)

Stoked? Not exactly. Unless "stoked" suddenly meant "miserable."

jujuBEE: Harl? u there?

harliegirl95: yeah, I'm here.

gOalgirl: aren't you Xcited? :):)

harliegirl95: dunno

JUSTme713: how come, H?

jujuBEE: u r not happy about the baby?

IzzyBELLA: i wish my mom was having a baby. Little
babies r so cute!

harliegirl95: not sure how I feel yet. Gotta get
ready for the bus.

gOalgirl: HARL, SOUNDS LIKE YOU NEED UR
PEEPS!!! I HEREBY CALL TOGETHER AN
EMERGENCY MEETING AT THE DOORZ!!!

jujuBEE: good idea, miss o. i'm in!

IzzyBELLA: me 2!

JUSTme713: I'll b there!

gOalgirl: Harlie????

harliegirl95: yeah, I think ur rite miss o. I really
need u guys 2day.

I didn't tell Lanie about the new baby—mostly because she didn't stop talking all the way to school this morning—but also because I wasn't sure I wanted her to know yet. She would just start asking a lot of questions about the baby, and I didn't feel like answering them yet.

When we arrived at school, I practically dragged Lanie to her class, just so I wouldn't be late for the "doorz."

"Bye, Harlie!" she called to me from her classroom. "Don't forget to save me a seat on the bus for the way home!"

As I raced back across the school toward the gym, I was happy to see that the buses were still lined up to drop off students. That meant I still had time to chat with the girls before the bell rang for class.

They were all waiting for me when I got there.

"Okay, Harlie," Miss O said before I could say a word. "We've all talked it over and we agree that you just need some time to get used to the idea of a new baby, and then you're going to be super-happy."

I shook my head. "I don't know, guys," I said. "The more I think about it, the more I realize that everything in my life is going to change! And not for the better!"

Juliette's voice was filled with concern. "What do you mean, Harlie?"

I tossed my book bag on the ground and leaned back against the doors. "Okay, look. A new baby. Sounds harmless, right?" I asked. "But do you have any idea what it means? I'm going to have to give up the Latte Lounge so the baby has somewhere to sleep!"

Isabella made a face. "Ooh. I hadn't thought about that," she said.

Miss O nodded. "Yeah, that does stink," she agreed.

"And it gets worse!" I told them. "They're painting over the mural, too! Dad said it wasn't exactly appropriate for a little baby!"

"Oh, no!" Miss O cried. "Our mural!"

"I know!" I agreed. "See? This is horrible!"

Miss O sighed. "It is pretty awful, Harlie," she said. "But honestly, it's not the end of the world. We can paint another mural, you know."

"I guess," I muttered.

"Yeah! We can paint it in your room!" Juliette suggested. "And it'll be even better than the first one!"

"Juliette is right," Justine said. "We can do the same thing in your bedroom. We'll all help!"

I sighed. "Thanks, guys. But that's not all."

Miss O's eyes narrowed at me. "What do you mean?" she asked.

"Well," I said, "to make room for the new baby, my parents need to clean out everything from the Latte Lounge. Everything that's mine, I mean! My guitar, my amplifier . . ."

"And your comic books?" Isabella asked gently.

I nodded. "Yup. They want to put them all away in a closet!"

"Get out!" Miss O cried. "Can't you just keep them in your room?"

"But where would I put them?" I asked her. "I have thousands of books. And a very small bedroom."

Justine put her hand on my shoulder. "Harlie, listen," she said. "We'll come over this weekend and help you rearrange your room. I just know we can find a place for all your stuff!"

"I don't know," I replied.

"Hey, I've packed and repacked a million times in my life!" Justine went on. "And I've had bedrooms of all different sizes and shapes! If anyone can find a way to fit thousands of comic books into a bedroom, it's me!"

I grinned. "I guess you're right," I said. "But that only solves half of my problems."

"What do you mean?" Miss O asked.

I gazed up at my friends, who were all looking at me with concerned looks on their faces. How could I possibly tell them what I was really thinking? That I was going to make a horrible big sister?

I had to tell someone. And after all, they were my best friends in the world. I knew I could confide in them.

"Here's the thing," I said. "I don't think I'm going to make such a great sister."

Miss O's eyes grew wide. "What are you talking about, Harlie? You are so great! You'll make an excellent sister!"

"Absolutely!" Juliette chimed in. "I saw how great you were the other day with Lanie! Even when she was, let's say, irritating, you still kept your cool! That's what great big sisters do!"

Miss O shot her a look. "Oh, really?" she asked. "Is that what you do when I'm, let's say, irritating?"

Juliette smiled. "You're never irritating!" she said sweetly.

"You better believe it!" Miss O joked.

I laughed at their silly argument, then I shook my head. "But what about the other day," I said, "when I yelled at Lanie for absolutely nothing?" I reminded them.

No one said anything.

"Remember? When she was just walking near my comic books? I yelled at her for no reason!"

"That wasn't so bad," Isabella commented. "You just overreacted a little. Everyone does that sometimes."

"I don't know," I said. "I just don't think I'm good with kids. I don't like playing with dolls, I don't like answering a million questions every day, and I don't like having to share my things!"

"Oh, come on, Harlie!" Miss O said with a grin. "You always share your stuff with us!"

"Yeah! Remember when you let me borrow your comic books?" Isabella reminded me. "You let me take them home for a few weeks to read when my ankle was in a cast! Those were some of your favorite books!"

"And you let me borrow your guitar pick necklace when I had a part in *Grease* last year," Justine added.

I nodded. "Yes, but you guys are my best friends in the world!" I said emphatically. "I love you guys!"

Miss O smiled. "But, Harl . . . you're gonna love your new sister, too!"

"It's true, Harlie," Juliette said. "I mean, sometimes it's not so great having a little sister. But most of the time it's a blast! Just wait until the baby gets here," she added. "You'll see!"

"That's another problem," I told them.

"What do you mean?" Justine asked.

"The baby," I said with a sigh. "She's coming in July. The same exact time as the Classic in Miami."

Nobody said a word.

"Which means," I explained to them, "that even if I qualify, I won't be able to go! My parents will never let me go to Miami when my mother is in the hospital having a baby!

"I'll have to drop out of the competition!"

Chapter 8

The Last Days of the Latte Lounge

On Saturday morning, I think my parents must have known I was feeling crummy because they were being annoyingly nice. Even Mom, who was still feeling sick in the mornings, offered to take me to Starbucks for my breakfast mocha latte.

As we walked back from Starbucks #27 on the list, Mom asked me about the baby.

"Are you excited even a little about being a big sister, Harlie?" she asked.

I sipped my latte and thought about how to answer that question. If I said "yes," I really wouldn't be telling the truth. But if I told the truth and said "no," it would crush her.

"I'm excited," I said, "but I'm also a little weirded out."

"Weirded out?" Mom asked in concern. "What does that mean?"

"Well," I began, "It means I need some time to get used to the idea. I guess it'll be cool to have another person in our family. But I'm not ready right now." That was truthful, at least.

"Okay," Mom said. "That makes sense. It's always been us three," she went on, "so I can see how adding another family member will take a lot of getting used to."

"Yeah. And all those changes," I said, taking another sip. "I can't stop thinking about how my whole life is going to be different."

"But Harlie, I told you I'm going to try my best to keep everything the same. As normal as possible."

"Mom, you can't keep everything the same," I told her.

"Your father and I can try," she insisted. "I mean, I know we're asking you to give up your Latte Lounge, and that means a lot to you. But we'll make it up to you somehow, Harlie."

We had just arrived at our building, and Carli, the weekend door-woman, held the door open for us.

"Mom, you can't make it all up to me!" I said. "How could you possibly? The baby is coming, there's no changing that. I have to give up my Latte Lounge and a whole bunch of other things. I have to change my whole life!"

As soon as those words came out of my mouth, I felt as if I were going to burst into tears. I guess I had a lot of stuff building up inside of me that I hadn't realized.

How could my parents keep telling me everything was going to stay the same? That the new baby wasn't going to change my life? That was crazy. The new baby was going to change everything.

And didn't she see just how much I was giving up? It wasn't just about the Latte Lounge, it was about so much more! It was about the Classic and my gymnastics training and my weekends in Chinatown with my dad and my trips to Starbucks with my mom. The new baby was going to ruin all of it!

I pushed the elevator button as many times as I could, hoping that would make the elevator come faster. If Mom saw me crying, that would be the end of it. She'd want to have a big family meeting to discuss my feelings over and over and over. I didn't think I could handle that.

"Harlie, are you crying?" Mom asked me, her voice filled with concern.

I bit my bottom lip to keep from shedding any tears. "No, I'm not!" I choked. "I just don't want to talk about the baby anymore, okay?"

We stepped into the elevator and rode up to our floor in silence. All I wanted to do at the moment was lock myself up in my room and play the guitar. The girls were coming over in an hour, and I didn't want them to see me upset.

When we got up to the apartment, I stepped inside and found Dad in the living room chatting with Mrs. Kappel. Lanie was on the carpet, playing with Rocky.

"What's going on?" I asked. I wiped my eyes on my sweatshirt sleeve, just in case they were still watery.

"Hi, Sugar Plum," Dad said. "While you were out, Mrs. Kappel came by. I think she needs to ask you a favor."

"Hello, Harlie!" Mrs. Kappel said. "I do need a favor! A big, big, big favor!"

Uh-oh. Please don't make it involve babysitting!

"A client of mine is in the midst of an emergency, and I promised I would go help her this morning," Mrs. Kappel said. "But they have cats, and Lanie is scared of cats, so I can't bring her along. Mr. Kappel is at a breakfast appointment and won't be back until after lunch. Would you mind if Lanie stayed with you until then?"

Ack! It *is* a babysitting favor! The last thing I want to do right now is deal with Lanie!

"Well, um, I kind of have plans this morning," I said hesitantly. "My friends are coming over in a little while. I'm really sorry, Mrs. Kappel."

Mrs. Kappel smiled. "You don't have to apologize, Harlie. It's okay. I'll work something else out. I know I asked last minute and all."

As she stood to leave, I happened to catch sight of Lanie's face and I felt very guilty. You should have seen how sad she looked!

"G'bye, Rocky!" I heard her whisper. "I'll play with you another day, okay?"

I watched as Rocky slowly rose from his comfy position on the floor and rubbed up against Lanie. I couldn't believe it—he usually only did that to me!

Then Lanie gave Rocky a big hug. And he whimpered. Can you believe it? He seemed to know what was going on and that Lanie was leaving!

All at once I felt horrible about telling Mrs. Kappel that I couldn't watch Lanie. What was the big deal anyway? I mean, I could still hang out with my friends even if Lanie was here. She could keep busy playing with Rocky. From the looks of things, Rocky would love it, too.

As it turned out, my dad was thinking the same thing.

"Honey," he said, "can't Lanie hang out with you and the girls for a little while? It won't be for too long."

I nodded. "I guess that would be okay," I said. "Mrs. Kappel, it'll be okay if Lanie hangs out here this morning."

Her eyes widened. "Are you sure?" she asked me. "I don't want to put you out."

"It's no problem," I assured her. "We were just going to hang in my room anyway," I explained. "Lanie can hang with us, or she can hang with Rocky if she wants."

Lanie's eyes were brighter than sunshine as she looked up at me with a ginormous smile. She could sure be cute sometimes. But I knew better. I knew that behind that angelic face there was a temper tantrum just waiting to explode. I also knew that there was no way I was going to go through that again!

If Lanie was going to hang with me and my peeps today, there were some ground rules that needed to be discussed first!

"Give me a sec to have a private chat with Lanie," I told Mrs. Kappel. "We'll be right back." I led the five-year-old into the living room and out of earshot from our parents.

"Here's the deal, Lanie," I told her. "You want to hang out here today, right?"

Lanie nodded enthusiastically. "Yes!" she said.

"Okay then. But you have to make me a promise."

"Okay! I promise!" she declared instantly.

I let out a laugh. "Well, you have to wait to hear what the promise is first!"

"Oh, okay."

"So, here's the deal. If I agree to let you hang out with the girls and me today, and let you play with Rocky as much as you want, you have to promise me that you won't be annoying and ask a million questions all day. And most importantly, you have to promise you won't stomp your foot at me, or have a temper tantrum when it's time to go."

Lanie nodded again. "Okay!" she said. "I promise!"

Hmmmm. That was too easy.

"Lanie, I mean it!" I told her. "When the playdate is over, it's over. No tantrums and no begging to stay longer or anything."

"Okay! I promise!" she said again. "Really truly!"

I thought for a moment. "Then pinky swear," I said finally.

Lanie's eyes narrowed. "What does that mean?" she asked.

"You don't know about pinky swearing?" I asked.

Lanie shook her head.

"Well, that's how my best friends and I make promises to each other," I explained. "We lock pinkies like this,"

I locked my pinky around hers.

"And then we make the promise and pull our pinkies apart like this."

I gave a tug, then released her pinky.

"After you pinky swear," I told her, "there's no breaking the promise under any circumstances! Understand?"

Lanie was listening intently, hanging on my every word. She nodded. "Okay!"

"So if you pinky swear with me, like I do with Miss O, Juliette, Justine, and Isabella, you really, really have to mean it!"

"I mean it!" she cried. She locked pinkies with me again. "I promise! No questions! No tantrums! I pinky swear promise!"

I grinned and put my arm around her shoulders. "Good," I said. "Now let's go tell your mom you'll be hanging out with me this morning."

A little while later, Miss O stood in the middle of my bedroom and gazed around at the space we had to work with. Well, to be more exact, the lack of space!

Isabella, Justine, and I were hanging out on my bed, and Juliette was at my desk, spinning in my chair. Lanie and Rocky played tug-of-war on my carpet with Rocky's favorite pink rope toy.

"I think we can do it!" Miss O declared cheerfully. She scooped up a handful of M&Ms from the jar of M&Ms I kept on my desk and popped some in her mouth. "If we put your bed and your dresser against the wall with the windows," she said as she munched, "there would be enough room on the other wall for the mural."

"But what about Harlie's comic book collection?" Isabella pointed out.

"Right now it's on the bookshelf in the new baby's room. We can't fit that big bookshelf in this room."

"Hey, I know!" Juliette said, looking at me. "How about if you and the new baby switch rooms?"

I sighed and reached for some M&Ms, too. "Nope," I said, tossing some in my mouth. "Already thought of that. But my mom said the baby's nursery has to be in the Latte Lounge because it's closest to her bedroom. You know, so when the baby wakes up at night she and my dad can hear her."

"Darn," Juliette said disappointedly. "I thought I had the perfect solution!"

I grinned at her. "It was a good idea, Juliette. It's just that I tried suggesting it already. Keep thinking."

"Well, if we move the bed the way Miss O said," Justine offered, "and put your dresser right next to it, then we can fit the Harlie Rox mural on the wall next to the door. That would leave room for the comic books over on the other wall."

"That might work," I considered. "But the bookcase still won't fit in here."

I suddenly noticed that Lanie, who had been sitting on my carpet the whole time as quiet as can be, was raising her hand and rocking back and forth on her knees as if she were in school and needed to ask the teacher an important question.

I giggled. "Lanie, why are you raising your hand?" I asked.

"Because I have a question," she replied. "And I didn't want to be annoying."

Miss O laughed. "You're not being annoying, Lanie," she said.

"You can ask me a question!" I told her. "When I told you all that before, I didn't mean you had to sit there all day in total silence, silly!"

"Oh. Ooops," Lanie said.

"No problem. So what's your question?" I asked.

"Actually, it's an idea," Lanie said.

"Great! We need ideas. Shoot!" I said.

"Okay. Well, my daddy used to keep his baseball cards in boxes," Lanie explained. "He has a collection, too, just like you, Harlie. But Mommy said the boxes looked shabby."

"Lanie's mother is a decorator," I told the girls.

"An interior decorator," Lanie corrected me.

"Right. An interior decorator."

"So Mommy bought these pretty plastic boxes for all of his cards. He filled them up and then he put the boxes on top of each other and made a table!"

My eyes widened. "Lanie! That is an awesome idea!" I exclaimed.

Lanie smiled. "And then you can keep your comic books in mint chocolate chip condition!" she added proudly.

Everyone laughed.

"You mean mint condition?" I asked.

Lanie's face reddened. "Yeah," she said. "Mint condition. The plastic boxes will keep them in mint condition."

"You're a hundred percent right, Lanie!" Juliette told her. "And I know where we can get the coolest boxes! In hot pink and Day-Glo colors!"

"Wow, that would be perfect!" Miss O gushed. "Then we could store your comics in boxes that match the mural!"

"Oh, and how about this idea?" Justine offered. "You can put the boxes together to make a coffee table for in here!"

"No! A latte table," Isabella joked.

"What cool ideas! I love it!" I cried. I turned to Lanie. "Thanks, Lanie! You're a genius!"

Lanie smiled from ear to ear. Then she went back to playing tug-of-war with Rocky as the girls and I went into the Latte Lounge. We sat down on my beanbag chairs and tried to figure out how many plastic boxes I would need for all my comics.

"I think the boxes are about this big," Juliette motioned with her hands. "So I bet you could fit all your comics in twelve boxes. Then you can put six on the bottom—three in a row and three in a row next to them. Then put a box on top of each box and you'll have a coffee table . . . I mean a latte table."

"Do you really think it'll work?" I asked her.

Juliette nodded. "Sure," she said. "It's worth a try anyway. If it doesn't, you'll still have some very funky storage boxes for your books!"

"True," I said. "Okay, let's go back to my room and see how much money I've saved from babysitting. I wonder how much the boxes cost. I hope I have enough for twelve of them."

My parents walked past us just then. Dad was carrying a basket of laundry, and Mom was pushing a cart filled with more laundry and detergent.

"Honey, we're going down to the laundry room in the basement to use the machines," Mom said. "Our machine isn't working. We'll be back in just a few minutes. Think you can handle things?" she asked with a wink.

"I think so," I joked. "But Dad, can you walk us to the store after lunch?" I asked. "I need to get some storage boxes for my room."

"Sure, Sugar Plum," he replied.

"Great! Thanks!"

Back in my room, I found my piggy bank under my bed. It's not really a piggy bank—I just call it that because I keep all my money in it. It's actually a wooden box that I decorated at camp last summer. I flipped open the top and dumped all the money onto my bed.

As I counted my cash, Miss O and Isabella began setting up the projector in my room, while Juliette and Justine began moving the junk I had by my door into my closet to make room for the mural.

I had counted up to thirty-two dollars and eighty cents when I happened to glance over at Lanie. She and Rocky had finished their game of tug-of-war, and now Rocky was chillin' on his back while Lanie rubbed his tummy. Rocky was in doggie heaven: He loved having his tummy rubbed! I have to say, it was really nice to see those two getting along so well.

As I watched Lanie with Rocky, I happened to notice something else. It was Lanie's arm—the one she was using to pet Rocky. There were bright red blotches all over it!

"Lanie! What's the matter with your arm?" I asked in alarm.

That's when I realized that Lanie seemed kind of sleepy. I called out to her again, and she could barely turn her head to look at me! In a panic, I dropped my money and rushed over to her. I pulled her chin toward me and took a look at her face. I freaked—her face was bright red, and her eyes were starting to swell!

"Holy Moley!" I cried. Without missing a beat, I flew into the living room and grabbed the cordless phone.

As quickly as I could I dialed 9-1-1.

Chapter 9
Nine-One-One

"West Ninety-first Street!" I quickly told the operator. "Fourth floor, apartment J."

My stomach was doing flip-flops and my hands were shaking like crazy as I spoke to the 9-1-1 operator. I could barely remember my address when she asked me for it!

"Miss, can you describe the young girl's arms and face," the operator asked.

I gulped nervously. "Um, her arms have bumps on them. And they are red," I said, trying to sound as calm as possible. Lanie was now lying on my bed, and I was sitting right by her side. I didn't want to sound scared or anything when I spoke to the operator because it might frighten Lanie.

"And her face is red," I went on. "It's not so bad, except that her eyes are swollen. Very swollen. And she's kind of sleepy-like," I added.

"Okay, an ambulance is on its way. I'll stay on the phone with you until it arrives." the operator said calmly.

Lanie looked at me through her puffy eyes and I could see through the swelling that they were teary, too.

"I don't feel good, Harlie!" she mumbled. "I'm sorry!"

I picked up her hand to hold it. "Lanie! What are you sorry about?" I asked.

"Because I'm bothering you," she said. "And I promised to be good." Then she started to cry for real.

"You are good, Lanie!" I told her. "This isn't your fault! You're sick!"

"I'm scared!" she said breathlessly.

Me, too, I thought to myself.

I glanced toward the bedroom door for my friends. "Did Juliette and Justine go to get my parents?" I called out.

Miss O raced into the room. "Yes!" she told me. "They should be on their way up!"

I took a deep breath and exhaled to calm my nerves. Where was that ambulance already? Then I remembered I was still on the phone with the operator.

"Will the ambulance be here soon?" I asked her.

"Yes, sweetheart," she assured me. "They are pulling up to your building right now. You should tell them everything you told me."

"Okay, thank you." I replied. Then I leaned over Lanie and whispered in her ear to let her know the ambulance had just got here.

Lanie could barely move.

I smoothed her bangs off her face and wiped her tears away with my shirtsleeve. "You're going to be fine, Lanie," I told her gently. "I think you're having an allergic reaction to something. A kid in my class once had the same thing. It looked just like this. I called your mom's cell, and she's on her way, too."

"Am I allergic to Rocky?" Lanie managed to ask.

"No, I don't think so," I told her. "This would have happened before. You've played with him lots of times. It has to be something else. Are you allergic to anything that you know of?" I asked.

"Just peanuts," she said, sounding out of breath. "But I didn't eat any peanuts."

That's when I noticed the jar of M&Ms on the floor. I never leave it on the floor—I always keep it up high on my desk because of Rocky. Chocolate makes dogs very sick—and since Rocky loves to eat, I wouldn't put it past him to sniff out my M&M stash.

"Did you have any M&Ms?" I asked her.

Lanie nodded slowly. "Two," she said. "But not the peanut ones."

So that can't be it either, I thought. I checked Lanie's arms again, and they were even bumpier than before. Plus, her neck was starting to turn red and blotchy, too. Then she reached up to her throat, complaining that it was getting hard to breathe. My heart thumped in my chest.

Please, oh please! I begged. Let her be okay! Don't let anything happen to her!

Luckily, my parents came running into my room at that exact moment.

"Poor thing!" my mother exclaimed. "Don't worry, Lanie, the doctors are on their way up!"

"Should I wait for them by the door?" I asked. But when I moved to get up, Lanie pleaded with me to stay.

"No! Don't go, Harlie! Please stay with me!" she cried. All I could think about was oh my god, what if something terrible happened to her?

I sat back down on the bed and lifted her little head onto my lap. "I'll stay right here with you the whole time," I said. I could see how scared she was. "I promise!"

Lanie struggled to take a breath. "Pinky swear?" she managed to say.

I felt tears come to my eyes. "Pinky swear," I whispered in her ear.

Chapter 10
Big Sister,
Here I Come!

I was the only one Lanie would let hold her while the EMS doctor gave her a shot. It was a big, big needle, too—I think I would have been running for the hills if it had been me getting that shot! But Lanie was really brave. All she wanted was for me to hold her. (Or maybe she was so "out of it" she didn't even notice the needle.)

Anyway, I wrapped my arms around her and she buried her head in my shoulder. Then I whispered in her ear and tried to think of something funny to say to take her mind off the shot.

"You know," I whispered, "I'll bet you're not feeling like you're in 'mint chocolate chip condition' right now."

"Heh," she said softly.

Was that a chuckle? I wondered.

Okay, she may not have been in any shape to laugh, but at least she had stopped crying and said "Heh." That was a good sign anyway.

I watched as they gave her the needle. I forgot what the doctors called it exactly, but it sounded like, "epi pen." It was for really bad allergic reactions. I held on to Lanie a little tighter and stroked her hair as the needle went into her leg.

"Almost over," I whispered.

Lanie didn't even cry.

By the time Mrs. Kappel flew through the front door about ten minutes later, Lanie was sitting next to me on the sofa in my living room, looking as happy as a clam and brushing Rocky's fur. The doctors were packing up their equipment, and the air was calm, but I'm sure the sight of a hospital stretcher and several emergency medical technicians in my living room totally freaked Mrs. Kappel out. Luckily, my mother met her at the door and calmly reassured her that Lanie was going to be okay.

Lanie's mom raced to her side and hugged her real hard. Too hard, actually. I know this because Lanie looked at me and made a funny face with crossed eyes while it was happening.

I laughed quietly. I was starting to feel a little better. Ten minutes ago though, I thought I would pass out.

That had been the scariest thing ever. My heart was still thumping like crazy in my chest, even though the EMS doctor—his name was Jordan— had said Lanie was going to be just fine.

We figured out that Lanie must have accidentally eaten a tiny piece of peanut that was left over in my candy jar and mixed up with my plain M&Ms. It had, I guess, been in there since the last time I had peanut M&Ms. Lanie thought she'd only eaten plain M&Ms, but Jordan had found a small piece of peanut stuck in her back teeth. She must have scooped it up with the plain M&Ms without knowing it.

Before he left, Jordan came over to the sofa to check on Lanie one last time.

"Looking good, Little Lady!" he said cheerfully.

"Thank you," Lanie said.

"Remember, no candy without inspecting it first," he warned.

"Okay," she promised. "I pinky swear."

"You're one lucky girl," he added as he headed out the door. "Thanks to your quick-thinking big sister, you're going to be just fine!"

I almost burst out laughing. Big sister?

I turned to see a huge grin on Lanie's face.

"He thought you were my sister!" she said with a chuckle. "That would be so cool!"

I smiled. "Yeah, it would be cool," I agreed, giving Lanie a quick hug.

Mrs. Kappel pulled me away from Lanie and squeezed me until I thought I would pass out. Her eyes were all wet from crying, and there was black stuff running down her cheeks from her makeup.

"Harlie, Harlie, Harlie!" she cried. "I can't thank you enough! You saved my little girl's life!"

I blushed. "You're welcome," I said meekly. "But I think I was more scared than she was," I admitted.

"You didn't show it at all, Harlie," Miss O said.

My friends all nodded in agreement.

"You knew just what to do," Juliette commented. "I don't know if I would have known what to do."

"Me, either," Justine said. "You took charge and totally saved the day!"

"You must be so proud of your daughter," Mrs. Kappel said to my parents. "What a responsible young woman! I can never thank her enough." Then she started to cry again, and her makeup got even worse.

"Thank you," my mother said. "We are very proud of her." As she consoled Mrs. Kappel, Mom winked at me and whispered, "I guess you were wrong about something."

"What's that?" I asked.

"About being ready to be a big sister," she said.

I nodded.

Yes, I was agreeing with her. After today, I didn't think I would ever feel the same way again. I mean, technically, I wasn't a big sister yet. I know that. But after all that had happened, I really felt like a big sister!

Best of all, now when I think about the new baby coming, I don't get that uncomfortable, yucky feeling deep down inside. The feeling that I wouldn't know what to do with a sister or how to act with her or play with her.

Now I realize I do know all those things! In fact, at the moment, I already felt like an old pro!

"This calls for a celebratory sleepover!" I announced after Lanie and her mother had gone home and it had quieted down in the apartment.

"And what are we celebrating, exactly?" Isabella asked.

"Um, hello? I just saved someone's life?" I reminded her.

Isabella rolled her eyes. "Oh, right. That."

I punched her playfully in the arm. "Ha! Do you think your parents will let you?" I asked.

"Yeah, I think so. It's Saturday, so it should be fine." Isabella said.

"I think we can stay, too." Juliette chimed in.

"I'll call and ask," Justine said, "but it should be okay."

I looked over at my mother. "Mom?"

She laughed. "How nice of you to ask me!" she joked.

"Sorry!" I said with a giggle. "But is it okay?"

"Of course it is," she said. "But your father can make dinner tonight. I've had enough excitement for one day!"

That night, I couldn't stop laughing.

We were acting all silly and stuff, especially Juliette, who kept pretending to faint just so I would call 9-1-1 again. She said she had a major crush on Jordan the EMS doctor.

Mom let us eat pizza in my bedroom that night, which was so cool. And the best part was the pizza boxes and our plates were all on top of my new, awesome, hot pink latte table! After that thing with Lanie, my dad had walked the girls and I over to the store to buy the plastic boxes. We had spent the next few hours putting all my comics into them. And they all fit perfectly! Then we stacked them up in the middle of my room and made a super-funky, cool latte table.

"Hey, what are your parents going to name the new baby?" Miss O asked as we munched on our pizza.

I shrugged. "I don't know," I replied.

"Can we make a list of cool names?" Isabella asked.

"Yeah, sure," I said. "I'll give it to my parents and see what they say."

"I like Cameron," Miss O said. "That's my favorite name."

"Mine is Shannon," Isabella piped in.

"For a girl, I like Tia," Justine added.

Juliette smiled dreamily. "How about Jordan?" she asked.

I threw a pillow at her. "You're pathetic!" I cried.

Just then, my mother stuck her head in my room. My dad was standing next to her. "Harlie, you have a phone call," she said, tossing me the phone.

"Who is it?" I asked.

"Coach Saffeir," she replied.

Everyone in the room grew quiet. Coach Saffeir calling could only mean one thing: I was about to learn the results of the Classic qualifying meet.

I took a deep breath and picked up the phone.

"Coach Ilana?" I said. "Hi!"

I listened in silence as everybody hung on my every word.

"Wow, that's great!" I said excitedly. I gave them all the thumbs-up. My friends hugged each other and did a quiet celebratory dance.

Then I looked over at Mom and I thought about the decision I had made just a few short hours ago. I hadn't told it to anyone yet. Not to my best friends, or to my parents. Now I was about to, and boy were they going to be surprised.

"Coach Ilana? I'm really happy about qualifying," I told her. "But I'd like to give my spot up anyway."

Everybody stopped celebrating and stared at me in shock. The room was so quiet, I swear I could hear my heart beating!

"I can't be in the Classic this July," I explained to my coach, "because I don't want to be way across the country when my new baby sister is born."

My mother put her arm around my shoulders. "Harlie, you don't have to do that," she said. "I know how much the Classic means to you!"

"Your mother is right, Sugar Plum. This is too important to miss!" my father added.

I said goodbye to Coach Ilana, hung up the telephone, and shook my head. I thought I would feel really, really sad after dropping out of the competition, but oddly, I didn't feel sad at all.

"There will be other Classics," I told my parents, giving them both a big hug. Then I patted my mother's little pregnant belly. "It's this," I said, "that is too important to miss!"